The
Devil
Brigade

by Toni Odell

Printed in the United States of America
First printing: 2013
ISBN: 0615919340
ISBN-13: 978-0615919348

Cover Art Design: Marissa Letterio.
Copyright © 2013 Oddite Delight Design.

Fair Moon To Thee I Sing, by Arthur Sullivan and W.S.
Gilbert. From H.M.S. Pinafore, 1875.

Zadok Books
PO Box 337
Hughsonville, NY 12537

www.ToniOdellBooks.com

For Frank Mercer

ACKNOWLEDGMENTS

This has been a hell of a ride and I needed some folks to buckle me in. First and foremost, I have to say thank you to Christina Ventura - DiPersia, Sara Ventura, Dom Cuccia, Stephanie Rugar, Chris Davis, Melissa Magnolia, Ryan Seedorf, Jeanette Sayago, and Yonni Groza for the support I needed to get this project off the ground. I also have to give a shout out to everyone on Indiegogo who contributed. Every dollar counted and you guys are what keep indie writers alive and well.

Thanks to John and Karen Odell, my lovely folks, who smiled through gritted teeth when I told them I wanted to drop my Education classes to major in Creative Writing. You guys will get that beach house one day. On the other side of the family, I need to say thanks to James for all the sci-fi chats at the dinner table and Connie for dealing with my quirks and letting me borrow her son for awhile.

A big shout out to Frank Mercer for reading the drafts and dealing with my neurotic mess of a brain sometimes (and for all the reassurance and cups of tea.)

Marissa Letterio, thank you for the awesome cover, the years of friendship, and the introduction to Evil Dead. Without you, I might have been writing

Twilight and 50 Shades fan fiction somewhere...

Tom Waits: Thanks for putting all those monsters in my brain and providing me with music that my friends hate.

Wikipedia: Thanks for giving the world the glorious gift of The Random Article Button. Without it, I never would have gotten the inspiration for the original (yet awful) concept for this series.

But I need to shout out the most important thank you of all: You, the reader. You are what makes this all worthwhile. Your support means the world to me. Thank you and I really hope you'll be back again for some more macabre adventures with me. Ride or die, kids.

Love and explosions,

Toni Odell
Wappingers Falls, NY
October 11, 2013

CHAPTER 1

Ringmaster stepped out from behind a fringed curtain and twirled his cane between long, crooked fingers. The wooden piece spun fluidly, helicoptering back and forth from thumb to pinky in the dead, humid air. It was Saturday and it was just about time for the first show of the night. His dark, penciled-in eyes seemed to sparkle as he cleared his throat and barked out a deep, booming call. "Step right up, step right up. Ladies and gentlemen, strangers and friends, why don't you come close and stay for awhile? The Devil Brigade is here!"

His cane's spinning stopped and the end flipped back behind him as he lowered himself into a long, dramatic bow, arms straight out to his sides and his head down by his hips. When he pulled himself back up, there was not a soul watching. Around him, men and women strolled past his stage, dust rising from the dead country grass under their thick boots. They all seemed to ignore the sickly green banner slung across the stage from frame to frame: "Freak Show of the 19th Century - presented by Ringmaster Tom!" The stage was held up with large, swollen wooden poles and filthy curtains that obscured most of the rotted wooden floor. Whether or not they ignored him or just were not interested, the crowd was all the same, filled with men in long shirts and black hats and women with fluffed, short sleeves fanning themselves. They kept their heads turned away from blood red posters splattered with strange and grotesque bodies posed in awkward positions like melted wax statues. Phrases like "Leave your disbelief at home!" and "Those faint of heart - keep walking!" lined the disturbing images.

Ringmaster removed his oversized black top hat and scratched at frizzy white hair that pointed wildly in all directions. He rolled the hat back and forth between his fingers in the same motion as his cane, magically spinning the tattered thing like a basketball. As he spun the hat in deep thought, watching the men and women ignore the stage, he wondered which act would be the best to catch the crowd by surprise, but not climax too quickly. This town didn't seem like much of a freak show kind of place - they were hardened, tired people who needed fun and excitement to help them forget their factory jobs and starving children, not the weird and macabre arts. For Ringmaster Tom, it was art just to keep the fans engaged, to give the best performance every night without losing stragglers and families pulling away one by one. It took him years to master his technique and perfect the opening and closings: those moments that were remembered far more than the middle. His freaks were some of the best this year and he knew that any one of them would be a decent introduction, but who would be best for last? The Throwaways tonight were a decent bunch, strange freaks he found locally that could breathe life into the act. Maybe he could stage them last, or maybe filter them throughout his traveling show.

He knew that before he could do any of that, he needed to draw some eyes to the stage. What good is a freak show without the gasps and awe? He stepped loudly and deliberately across the platforms of the stage, each boot step thudding and echoing. The hat continued to roll in his fingers. He needed the perfect catch to call out to, someone charming and engaging to intrigue passing eyes and keep them stopping, one after the other.

As if on cue, a young woman in a frilly white dress stepped up to the side of the stage. Her skirt bounced heavenly among the lanterns that lit the carnival night. Her face was round and sweet, a lost cherub in this sad town. Her hair was in tight blonde curls that snapped back and forth around her neck and down the front of her lacy, white blouse. Not a single speck of the park seemed to cling to her and she stood radiantly among the sad, tired faces. She held a wispy mound of fairy floss candy as she stared at the poster on the front of the stage. The image was covered in black, bold question marks and words that asked, "Who is Bubonic Boy?"

Her head cocked to the side and she took a bite of her candy as she read. Ringmaster stared at her and wondered if his prayers had been answered. She would be perfect for catching eyes.

He stopped pacing and knelt down in front of her, a few feet above her thick blonde curls. He put his top hat back on his head and pressed his cane into his multicolored coat, addressing her with a respectful bow. "My, my, my! What a beautiful girl! I've been all over the world and have never seen such beauty as yours!"

He smiled a charming smile and realized she, in fact, was abnormally beautiful. Almost like a doll, unrealistically large blue eyes and porcelain skin that radiated under the moonlight. She smiled back at him flirtatiously and giggled.

He was caught off guard by her receptiveness but continued to croon. "Who brought such a lovely young lady here tonight?"

She looked behind herself shyly, then back up to Ringmaster. "Nobody. Just me tonight."

He continued to hold his smile as he removed his cane from inside his coat jacket and on the top of the cane's knob a small white dove sat, fluttering its wings. "It's never smart to let a little birdie be by herself...she could fly away!" He shook the cane and the dove startled and flew.

The woman pointed up at the bird and laughed. "Wow! How did you do that?!" A few turned their heads and looked at her, then up at the bird she pointed to. They stopped moving and began to listen and watch. Ringmaster's voice got a little louder.

"I've learned many things in my travels, my dear. Will you be so kind as to stay awhile and see what else I have discovered?"

"Sure! I would love to. Something tells me this will be a fun show."

A few others began to stand in front of the stage and with one stopped person, another stopped and the gathering began. They murmured and pointed at the signs and posters curiously, the hum of the crowd rising. Ringmaster waited until he counted fifty or sixty heads. He was in disbelief of how quickly she brought in a crowd. *If I could only have a type like her at every show, I'd be doing the best business of my life,* he thought.

He adjusted his top hat, cleared his throat, and opened his mouth to address his waiting audience.

* * *

Inside a dirty covered wagon sat a boy of no more than sixteen years old. He was among dishes, colorful props, boxes of costumes, and other various clutter. In his corner where he sat, he picked up a broken hand mirror and stared into it as he took a deep breath. He glared at the reflected fragments of himself, stretched this way and that, spotted and grotesque. He sighed and tried to think of what day it was. The crowd he heard Ringmaster conjuring suggested the business of a Saturday, but sometimes Friday could be busy too. The days seemed to all blur together after countless performances. His knees were sore and beginning to bruise, so he assumed he probably did some kind of stunt yesterday. It must be Saturday.

He knew it didn't make a difference. No matter the day or week or year, he would always do four shows a night. One show every hour. He would only be on stage for two minutes, sometimes three if the crowd loved him. Those minutes felt like hours, especially because he didn't have a choice. There were no sick days and no time off - he had to do what Ringmaster told him to and that was that.

The wagon he sat in was huge, although hardly large enough to carry the props and workers. It made him claustrophobic on long nights. At the moment, it was empty as the others were already behind the stage and ready for the first show of the night. They had pushed and nudged him to come along and wait, but he wasn't in the mood yet. His costume was simple and easy anyway - he could just grab everything and get up there a few minutes before he went on. He stopped caring if he was late because, if Ringmaster made a ruckus about it, he could play it up for suspense. At least that was always his excuse when it was brought into question and the whip was drawn.

The boy put down the mirror and glanced over at the flyer for the carnival. He wanted to read it from where it sat, but the candle light was too dim to make out any of the small words. All he could see were the large, print letters that said:

BUBONIC BOY: BLACK DEATH – ALIVE!

The letters were bold and black, standing out amongst the other images and phrases plastered across the paper. He knew underneath the title was a drawing of what he supposedly looked like. The drawing was horrific - a spotted creature with gigantic red eyes, a mouth curled in a snarl with rotted teeth and fangs exposed. Although he knew he didn't actually look like that, he couldn't help but feel there was some reality to it all. If he saw that creature wandering the streets, he would gasp and point just like the crowd gasped and pointed at him. He knew he could hold up the flyer to the candle to get a good look at it for the millionth time, but he asked himself what purpose it would serve except to make him more depressed.

Candles were the only source of light in the wagon, unless Ringmaster was feeling generous and would let them pull the cover of the wagon off a bit for some sunlight and air. He tended not to allow this for fear of others seeing the freaks outside of the show and starting terrible rumors. The boy wasn't exactly sure what could possibly be said that already hadn't been, but he took Ringmaster's word for it. He'd be doing this show forever, so he must know what's best.

The boy could feel the hot, dusty air blowing

through the holes in the wagon's canopy. He smelled sugary candy that probably tasted delicious. He never got the opportunity to try it, but the smell was always the same at every carnival and it always smelled nice and refreshing.

* * *

"My dear ladies, I don't believe you should take to the front stage now. Let the men protect you, just in case anything goes awry. I haven't seen a breakout since 1870 when Tarantula Man climbed the walls, but you can never be too safe."

The women in the front, who dusted off their skirts casually, looked up at Ringmaster with dull expressions and went right back to chatting amongst themselves. Everyone was half attentive in the crowd except for the beautiful young lady in the white dress who stared at him with a lovely smile. She had pulled further towards the back of the crowd, seated upon a stack of hay. He winked at her and prided himself with how well he wooed her, still in disbelief at her charm. She returned his affection with a soft smile.

"Well, you cannot say I didn't warn you, ladies! Welcome to Ringmaster Tom's 'Devil Brigade'. I've been running this show for forty years and I plan to do it for forty more. I've seen many oddities in my life, friends. I've seen things your eyes would not believe unless it came up and bit you right on the nose! And believe me, they will bite!" Ringmaster tapped at his nose for dramatic effect and paused for laughter. He received nothing but silence and a breeze of hot air.

"Eh, but never before have I owned freaks like these. It's been a good year for me, ladies and gentlemen. These are my best oddities yet! I've traveled the world to collect these living treasures and it gives me great pride to show you the bounty I've gained." Ringmaster stopped again, this time for applause. He saw bored eyes and a drunk who guffawed loudly. He clenched his teeth under his infinite smile.

"But why delay? Let us get to what you came here to see. Step right up, ladies and gentlemen! Step right up! The Brigade has arrived! We've much to conquer if we're to embrace our curious side, so let's start the show!"

Ringmaster bowed as the heavy curtain parted to reveal a metal cage behind him, splattered with brown and flaking blood. The thick bars of the cage were chewed and dented from top to bottom. "Don't be alarmed," he said, "The blood isn't human...at least, I don't think it's human. I always keep the safety of the audience at the forefront of my mind!"

Ringmaster grabbed one of the bars of the cage and spun the box around on its wheels, showing the pattern of large teeth marks and bites across it. A few members of the audience nudged each other and whispered curiously.

Ringmaster knocked on the cage with his cane with a quick rap, quieting the onlookers.

With the loud bang also came two pudgy, dark midgets - one male and one female - from each corner of the stage. They were dressed in loincloths and African war paint, white triangles and red circles across their cheeks and forehead. The male was shaved bald and the female had a tight, black ponytail centered at the top of her scalp. They came together side by side in the middle of the stage and stood to face the audience. Ringmaster smiled as he knelt between them, putting his hand on the top of the male's round little head. "Hot and Trot, my two lovelies here, come from the deepest bowels of the Congo River. They shot darts at my shins and kept me running after them for hours but with a quick scoop of a net, these two piggies were mine to have. With a little training and discipline, they're thoroughly obedient now. They will be my assistants for the evening, so let's give them a hand!"

Hot & Trot bowed together in perfect synchronicity. Several ladies clapped, but most stared blankly.

* * *

The boy slowly put on his costume, trying to delay the inevitable. He had five minutes until his set began and he had to take the stage. It was always these last few moments before he stepped on that gave him the most grief and worry. He was not feeling up to it, wishing he could just take a weekend off and be alone for once. As he buttoned up his heavy jacket, he thought about the sunlight and how he hardly ever got to experience it. He wondered if the others felt the same way as him, wishing they could just stop and breathe and take in the carnival setting. He wondered if they wanted to be humans too, or as close to human as they could get.

He never mentioned it to anyone because he knew it would make him look like the weakest link among them. The other freaks seemed so desensitized to the Brigade. All they did was work and sleep. They were so tough and ready to take the stage, much unlike himself. He didn't know how long they had been working for Ringmaster, but he never asked. He could only assume it was a very long time from their habits and clockwork schedules. For him, it never became second nature.

He knew that once he stepped foot on the stage he would be perfectly fine, though. He would do his little bit and get his cheers or boos. Sometimes the crowd would be in great spirits and they would clap so loudly that it warmed him and made him feel as if he were famous. Those were the moments that he didn't mind working.

Sometimes the audience would be disgusted and yell awful things until he left the stage and was out of sight. It was painful and embarrassing for him as he hid behind his costume. Whatever the crowd's outcome, he'd step off the stage after his few minutes of attention, return to the dark wagon, and sit and wait until he had to do it all over again.

As he stomped on his chunky boots and laced them up, he wondered how the crowd was going to be tonight. So far he hadn't heard much except some chattering and a drunk laugh, so it didn't seem entirely promising. He was always more comfortable when Ringmaster had them in his hand already by this point. The only good thing he did hear was a young woman that Ringmaster was talking to. She sounded sweet and had a nice laugh. Maybe she was pretty. He sighed and wiped the dust off the tip of his boots.

* * *

"The first creature we'd like to present to you today comes from the coldest lands of northeast Russia. He was one of the toughest fights I've had yet. I chased him through the deepest snows and harshest winds, following his strange, grotesque tracks halfway across the country. His speed and strength almost killed me, but with a little cunning he was mine for the taking. I'd like to introduce Werewolf, the hairy beast with the silver tongue!"

With a snap of his fingers, smoke shrouded the dented up cage behind him and misted across the stage. It caught in the wind and a few women coughed and waved it away, annoyed. Once the smoke dissipated, a tall, lanky body and long face appeared behind the steel bars, furiously shaking the cage. The figure was covered from head to toe in dark, coarse hair and his face was shrouded in thick clumps of what looked like fur. He wore an open dress shirt that was tattered and bloody, thick body hair protruding like wires from underneath. His eyes were large and blue like a wild dog as he growled and slammed his furry hands on the cage, shaking the flimsy trap. Some women gasped and a few men heckled. One man shouted, "Tell my wife to get off the stage!"

It sparked a few laughs amongst the audience and the chatter began to rise again. Ringmaster bit the inside of his cheek and cleared his throat abruptly. They quieted down and he continued his act.

"When I say silver tongue, I don't mean sarcasm and wit. No, no! This beast can barely grunt a word. But from what I've gathered from the local villages, Werewolf had once taken a local farmer's virgin daughter and did, well, quite unspeakable things to her. Once the father knew where this creature's mouth had been, he did what I'm sure all you gentlemen would do - ripped the beast's tongue out!"

Werewolf gnashed his teeth and opened his mouth, revealing a silver- plated tongue. A woman somewhere in the middle of the crowd shouted. "Aren't werewolves are vulnerable to silver?"

A few more laughs and jests rose amongst the viewers; even the young lady in the white skirt smirked a bit. Her look of skepticism seemed to ask him how he planned on getting out of this one...

Ringmaster coolly twirled his cane and pointed it at the woman, smiling down at her. "Ah, my dear. Your husband has been reading to you again, has he?"

She frowned.

"That's only of silly fairy tales and folklore. Not all that you read and hear is true. Tell me, how often have you seen werewolves and how are you so sure what they are and are not vulnerable to?"

She didn't speak.

"That's what I thought! Anyway, before he gets antsy, let us get him back to his regular cage so I do not have to chase him halfway across the globe once again."Another spout of mist shrouded the stage and werewolf lowered back down beneath the stage. Hot and Trot walked briskly to the right side of the curtain. Several audience members clapped and murmured amongst themselves and Ringmaster continued without delay before he lost the momentum.

"The next surprise I have in store for you is a little bit different. He won't fit in the cage, but you will not have to worry about your safety with this one. He can barely stand, let alone harm - as long as he's fed, that is! I'd like to introduce you all to The Commodore, the man the same size as his boat!"

Hot and Trot returned to the stage, struggling to pull a long wheeled table behind them. Across the top of it lay a sweaty, obese man with a black and gold Captain hat upon his bald head. Lumps of fat protruded out of his stretched and worn blazer decorated with little golden tassels and pins. His stomach rolled down towards his knees and over his thighs. His chubby fingers rested on the side of his bruised legs. Blue veins speckled calves the size of the midgets dragging him out. In one of his hands he held a half-eaten leg of turkey. Ringmaster walked a circle around him and held his own nose, his voice rising to a nasal pitch.

"What I have heard of our large friend here is that he was once the successful and handsome captain of the S.S. Sawyer. The boat had many successful tours until one day a terrible mistake had been made and the boat had struck another, killing all except for The Commodore here. He went into a state of sadness and rage and the only cure he could find was food. Years of guilt and gorging have made this man into a beast! Now, I've personally thought of removing Commodore from my show as I simply cannot afford the bill anymore. Full pigs, gallons of milk, and grand feasts is all he seems to enjoy. Isn't that right, sir?"

Commodore opened his mouth and bile poured down onto his shirt. The audience groaned and shrieked, pulling back in disgust. "Oh dear," Ringmaster said, shaking his head. "Let's get him back. I'm afraid he's gone and upset you."

Hot and Trot looked at each other, shook their heads as well, and struggled to push Commodore back off behind the side curtain. The applause was greater this time, the murmuring louder. Ringmaster took a small bow and did a quick scan of the audience. Shocked faces and laughter, the usual makings of a rising show. The young lady laughed and applauded as well and he couldn't help but smile back.

* * *

The applause pierced through the boy's thoughts and he realized it was starting to get too late. It was almost time for his act. He blew out the candle next to him, adjusted his mask, pulled the costume shut, and scooted off the wagon. *Just a few more times and then I get a whole day until tomorrow night. Unless it's Sunday... what day is it? I'll think about this later.*

* * *

Hot and Trot waddled back to the center of the stage and Ringmaster paced back and forth in front of them, addressing the audience in a deep, low voice. "I want you all to step back now. Yes, yes, please take a few steps back."

He waved his arms and hands at the audience, gesturing them backwards and they obliged, eying each other and the strange man on stage curiously. "Keep your distance from the Black Death: Alive! What was thought to be cured in the 14th century, we have the one and only known holder! Maybe he came to us from another time or maybe he has had it since birth, but one thing is certain. He is the walking nightmare of disease and pestilence and he simply will not die. Ladies and gentlemen, avert your eyes if you are weak to sights of disbelief and disfigurement. Men, hold your ladies and make sure they do not faint. Be prepared for a ghastly sight because unfortunately, in a world of modern cures and potions, nothing will fix this poor creature you're about to see."

Ringmaster paused and eyed the audience carefully. They were silent, hooked onto the suspense and waiting anxiously for his cue. He knew he had them right where he wanted them, so he adjusted his top hat and continued. " I found him on the streets of New York City. I know nothing about him as he does not speak. His lungs may be long disintegrated from his ailment. To think such a safe world would put such impending danger on us. For your entertainment, I present Bubonic Boy!"

* * *

Here we go.

From behind the curtain appeared a dark figure that took large, heavy steps towards the Ringmaster. The movement was slow, each step almost a stumble in scraping leather boots. It wore a long, black overcoat that dragged across the wooden stage. The head of the figure was a gigantic bird mask with clouded glass eye holes and a narrow, sharp beak. It turned from side to side, fluid and long in its motions like a pigeon. As the figure centered the stage, the audience remained silent and still, unable to take their eyes off it. Ringmaster peered across them, watching every breath they took.

The masked creature raised its hands and fumbled at buttons on the overcoat. Once they were all undone, the figure shrugged the overcoat off and revealed itself to be a thin, sickly young boy. His body was completely exposed except for very basic undergarments. The audience gasped in horror.

His legs and thighs were speckled black with boils and spots that looked like blood filled leeches. The blotches ran up and down his torso and arms, fingers curled and covered in black, chapped skin. His chest was thin and bony, ribs protruding, and his knees ready to buckle. He turned slowly, stomping to keep balance, showcasing his diseased shoulders and back.

The audience gasped and drew back, clamoring amongst themselves excitedly. Bubonic Boy stomped and turned again to face the crowd, but he lost his balance and fell forward towards the audience. A woman standing in the front screamed and backed into her husband, burying her face into his chest. He laughed nervously as he held his wife, but stepped backwards with her to get away from the creature on the stage, who now slumped down and curled up. He hid himself under his arms and hands and shook with shivers in the fetal position, sickly and dying.

Ringmaster waved his cane over the crowd again and gestured for them to stay back. "Be careful, ladies and gentlemen. We don't want this to spread. I would never wish this horror and pain upon you and the last thing we need is to start an outbreak all over again! Bubonic Boy is weak, you see – overridden by his powerful disease. I would like to bring him back into containment now, for everyone's safety. But before I do, would you like to see what's under the mask?

They all whispered to each other, suspicious and afraid. "Please don't!" a lady cried.

Ringmaster laughed and replied "Very well, my lovely. Hot, Trot - bring the boy back to his cage. We don't want to frighten these good people anymore."

Hot and Trot cautiously came out of the side of the curtain and slung the overcoat across Bubonic Boy's back. He put a hand on each of their tiny shoulders and hoisted himself up. The midgets walked alongside him as he stumbled to the back of the stage. There was a wave of relief across the audience and a sudden burst of applause. "Thank you, thank you," repeated Ringmaster with several bows. "If you think he's a sight, you're never going to believe what I have up next!"

* * *

As they carried Bubonic Boy off the stage, he whispered sharply to them, "Hurry up. This mask is hot as hell."

Hot and Trot picked up the pace and as soon as the boy's feet were behind the curtain they dropped his weight and he fell face forward with a large thump. The stage rose a few feet above the ground and he bounced down into the hard dirt. The mask thunked off the ground, knocking his head sideways, beak awkwardly pointing outwards. The boy felt dizzy from underneath the mask. "Thanks a bunch, guys."

He sat up and rubbed at his knee sorely, looking between the spots for any cuts or bruises, then glared up at Hot and Trot. Hot could only shrug.

The boy shrugged his arms into his overcoat and stood up, his body aching from the fall."Be gentle, guys. I bet you wouldn't like it if I just dropped you off the stage, too." He lifted each of the midgets off the stage and gently onto the ground, one by one. Trot nodded a thank you to him and spoke. "You ain't exactly light, Ben. You've got sixty pounds on the two of us combined, especially with that silly mask of yours." He spoke with a hard New York accent.

Ben shook his head and pulled the bird mask off. The hot air felt nice and cool after removing the dense leather from his face. His shaggy black hair fell across brown eyes and he slicked it all back with the sweat from his forehead. His face was devoid of spots except for the one his right cheek: a hairy mole of three inches protruding from his skin and deforming his otherwise handsome face. Ben sighed and said, "Alright. Let's get inside the wagon before anyone sees us, yeah?"

Hot and Trot nodded and the three of them ducked into the shadows of trees and banners until they were back into their wagon that they called home.

* * *

The young lady moved herself to the back of the crowd and could see, just beyond the curtain, a black haired boy and two little Africans hustle over to a wagon, scrambling inside. Her smile faded and her cherub aura was suddenly gone, her face now hard and unsettling. She looked up to the stage and saw Ringmaster bouncing happily to and fro, gesturing at the audience that stirred for him. She smirked to herself, brushed off her white skirt and walked away from the show, leaving the loud applause and hooting behind. Ringmaster never saw her leave.

CHAPTER 2

"Any bites today, sir?"

Andrew had a fishing net slung over his shoulder as he trotted into the muddy, dark lake. His slacks were rolled up over his knees and he had no shirt on, exposing his hairless body. Usually he would not dare to be seen in such little clothing, but it was late and dark except for a glow from a lantern. In the soft light he could see that someone was there with a fishing pole, jiggling the rod rhythmically. The boy took slow, intentional steps as to not disturb the other person's potential catch and watched curiously, realizing the man he spoke to never stirred at the sound of his voice. He seemed zoned out, completely unaware of his surroundings. Andrew peered his eyes to try and get a better glance at the stranger.

He was slender and lanky with a prominent statuesque face carved in neutrality. He was remarkably plain, wearing a dark, featureless jacket and slacks to match that were clean, but worn. He held an expensive fishing pole with a small sinker that dragged the line into the murky, but completely still water. The boy nervously shifted his eyes around to see if anyone else was beside them, but it looked like they were alone. The boy spoke again, this time a little louder, but still intent on not scaring away any fish. "Sir? Are you alright?"

The man jiggled the line harder, obviously annoyed at being bothered. Bubbles popped to the surface of the dark waters and then fell still. "I'm fine. Thank you." The voice was hoarse, as if he hadn't spoken in decades.

"Oh, okay then."

Andrew looked at the hard muscled face and the bright blonde hair that seemed unnaturally clean and healthy. It shone radiantly in the dim light. He began to feel uncomfortable looking upon the man for so long and glanced down at his feet. "I would come back tomorrow night as to not bother you sir, but we need the food. Do you mind my presence?"

Usually the boy was tougher than this, fighting off the bigger boys and claiming his territory, but something about the man bothered him and made him fearful. As if the man could feel the tension between them in the hot dusty night, he spoke again but this time softer. "No."

"Okay. Thank you, sir."

The boy stood calf-deep in the lake and quietly prepped the hook on his fishing line. He tried to stir as little as possible, hoping to become invisible to the man and not disturb him in the slightest. He wanted to look back over his shoulder and just stare, but he felt intrusive at even the thought of it.

The man jiggled the pole. "What's your name, child?"

The young boy cleared his throat nervously. "Ah, Andrew, sir."

"Andrew, a fisher of men." The man finally stirred a smile.

"Matthew 4:19. That's right, sir. My parents raised me religious, having read the Bible and such."

The man's eyes brightened and his hoarseness cleared. "You know how to read out here in the country?"

Andrew felt a nibble on the line and pulled back quickly, failing to set the hook as the line went limp. He sighed to himself. "The Bible is the only thing I've read," he responded as he watched jiggled the line again.

"If only one book to read, so be it. Be true to your name, boy."

The man stood and Andrew turned to look upon him. The man was much taller than Andrew thought he was and seemed vibrant and beautiful, even in his plain clothes. He could not speak, but only stare at the figure before him as if caught in a spell.

The man pointed into the distance. "You'll want to try the next lake over, down that long road. I'm sure you know the one - clearer waters than this. There hasn't been a bite here all night. Good night, Andrew. Take good care of your family."

Andrew could only nod stupidly as he watched the man step away, leaving his fishing pole and baits behind. Andrew thought to call to him and remind him he forgot his equipment, but began to realize that they were gifts. The man never mentioned it, but he could just feel it deep inside him that they were now his. He waded out of the water and back onto the ground, tossing his old pole aside. As he packed up his new finds, he started to think about blessings and miracles but ultimately found himself distracted by the shininess of the hook on the pole.

CHAPTER 3

Trot grunted and scrubbed at himself. "I hate washing this shit off."

He was leaning over a basin inside the wagon, washing the thick black paint from his face. As it dripped away, his white skin shone in patches. Beside him, Hot was doing the opposite and fixing her war paint for the next show, filling in her circled eyes. She glanced over at him and tsked. "Why do you do that," she asked. "You're going to have to put it on again in an hour. It's a waste of supplies and you know Ringmaster will have your head for it."

"So let him shrink it and call it a curio, then. I'm not going to suffocate from this stuff while he grabs another buck. He can spare a couple coins for paint."

Ben was sewing a hole in his faded overcoat, listening to their conversation with a smile on his face. "You want to talk about suffocating? Wear a plague doctor's mask and get back to me in ten minutes, let me know how you feel."

He scratched at the large mole on his cheek, irritated and red from the leather that bound the mask to his face every night. His skin always felt sweaty and clammy in the summer, like his deformities never seemed to give him any kind of painless break.

Hot snickered. "At least you can still see your skin, albeit spotty. Sometimes I forget what color I'm supposed to be..."

Ben, Hot, and Trot all shared a wagon together while The Commodore, being as big as he was, shared the larger trailer with Werewolf. They lived peacefully among one another, but it was because they had to. Commodore and Werewolf lived especially well together, but that was because Werewolf couldn't speak. He could only shrug his shoulders in response to anything Commodore said. The silver tongue was a prop that replaced the hole where his tongue was cut out. Rumor among the freaks spread that Werewolf had it removed by a Sioux Indian, but with no means to talk there was no way to confirm nor deny this. He would only shrug vaguely and leave the story at that.

Privacy was not something any of them were familiar with. They slept on cots side by side amongst the clutter of Ringmaster's stolen props, wardrobe chests, and supplies. There was no time to fight because they had to fix the props during the week and work all weekend. They would run out of town by Monday morning before any questions were ever asked about them and anyone even knew their real names. They were shadows in most towns, disappearing once it became dark in what seemed like ritual. Ringmaster told them it was for the mystery and intrigue of the show and to build a reputation before anyone could try and figure out the tricks and gimmicks of his acts, but Ben knew that it was really because Ringmaster would steal whatever he could and be miles away before anyone noticed. They always had a new prop to carry onto the wagon every weekend and it was certainly never a donation from the carnivals.

Ringmaster also hired local freaks he called "Throwaways." These were the strangers he picked up off the streets to perform for two nights. He would offer them obscene amounts of money and by payday he had already skipped town. The traveling crew never got to say two words to the Throwaways because Ringmaster "Didn't want them to get attached."

They were to be considered nothing more than a quick addition to the show and, according to him, the Brigade shouldn't speak to them for the sake of professionalism. "They may steal the brand and the secrets of the show if anything were to slip out," Ringmaster said all the time. They all knew it was bullshit, though. Mostly because everything he said tended to be bullshit. Ben always wondered how Ringmaster stole from everyone he met, yet could still find a new carnival for all of them to work every weekend.

He tied off a knot on the sewed up overcoat and held it up to admire his work. Over the years, Ben added numerous patches and handwork to the coat, giving it an unintentional bonus of creepiness. "How many Throwaways did Ringmaster bring on tonight?"
Hot squinted her eyes as she counted. "Uh. Three, I think. Siamese twins, a lady with no legs, and some guy with two....uh..."

Ben raised his eyebrows and snorted. "Wow. How's he going to pull that off?"

Trot laughed. "A pair of tight pants could do it, I suppose."

He raised his eyebrows at Hot and she blushed. Ben couldn't help but laugh. "Well, I guess it doesn't matter. He should be done in about twenty minutes, then."

He paused and felt that distinct nicotine craving pang deep in his stomach. He realized it had been hours since he last had a smoke and he probably would not have another chance if the crowds picked up. "I think I'm going to step out and have a cigarette behind the wagon before he gets back."

Hot shook her head at Ben as she said, "Probably not the best idea, honey. You know how Ringmaster gets. Just smoke in here."

"And smother myself? I don't think so. It's no big deal - I'll be in and out."

Trot put a hand on his hip and continued the lecture. "You know if he sees you, you'll never hear the end of it. Last time I got caught outside, he practically threw me across the wagon."

Ben shrugged. "Guess I'll have to make sure he doesn't see me, then."

He pulled on a pair of dirty, holey trousers and tapped his knuckles against the side of the wagon. "Do me a favor and knock if you see him coming."

Before he could be lectured anymore by Hot and Trot, he slipped out beneath the wagon cover and disappeared from their sight.

As the show continued and the cheers grew, Ben hid in the shadows of the trees and wagons. He slipped himself quietly beneath one of the heavy, wooden wheels and leaned up against it. There was plenty of room to stretch his legs and enjoy his cigarette in peace and solitude. As he took out his papers and tobacco from his pocket, he did what he always did when he had a moment to himself: got lost in his thoughts.

He didn't remember how he first met Ringmaster. He didn't really remember much of anything before the Brigade and working in the traveling freak show. There was no childhood or smiling parents or friends or schooling. Just one day he was on a wagon, his arms and legs speckled, traveling with a bunch of strange looking people eating bread and beans for dinner. They all seemed to know him, yet he had no idea who they all were. It was just how it was and he accepted it without asking questions.

Years had passed since that frightening night. The one time he tried to ask Ringmaster how he became part of the Brigade, he was answered with an angry glare and a gigantic story about being saved from the streets. "I put myself on the line to save you," Ringmaster yelled. "If it weren't for me, they would have burned you at the stake! Never forget what I've done for you, boy. I saved your life."

Ben had nodded and smiled appreciatively, but he didn't know what exactly not to forget. Sometimes he would get daring and try to ask for more information when Ringmaster was in a particularly decent mood, but the last time he did that he was answered with a whip and no dinner. He decided from that point on it was best to just accept it as it was and take the story at face value, occasionally thanking Ringmaster for the good that he had brought him, whatever it may be.

He knew that it didn't really matter where he came from since it was apparent he was abandoned anyway. At least his traveling crew was nice to him for the most part. He used to keep quietly to himself, but eventually Hot and Trot broke the ice for him and shared their cigarettes. He knew it was because they had to huddle together in a wagon every day and night, but at least they made the effort since they had no choice other than being friends.

He never knew why he was marked and scarred, either. He seemed like a healthy teenage boy, perfectly capable of breathing and walking and running. He just looked deathly. He was functional, but displeasing to look at, just like his companions on the road.

As he thought back on all of it, he lit a hand-rolled cigarette and sat within the shadow of the wagon wheel, inhaling deeply and enjoying the night air around him. He didn't know if it was healthy to think about this again, since it did nothing other than make him depressed and lonely. *How did the other guys do it,* he thought. *They seemed just fine...*

He heard a loud round of applause echoing from the stage in front of the wagon and Ringmaster's repeated, "Thank you, thank you, thank you!"

Ben sighed and took another hit on his cigarette, staring at the trees in the distance. His thoughts started to wander away peacefully. *Lots of woods and it's a hot summer...but not too hot.. Hmm. Are we in New York, maybe? The girls sound pretty. Could definitely be New York. Maybe I'm close to where Ringmaster found me..."*

A feminine voice sounded from behind him."Hey. I liked your show."

Ben coughed on the cigarette smoke in alarm. Frantically, he scrambled further underneath the wagon and hoped that whoever that was hadn't seen him. If Ringmaster found out he was outside of the trailer, he was going to be whipped and starved, if he was lucky.

He sat silent and motionless, hoping that she would walk away, but instead she giggled and said, "I already saw you. You might as well come out." The voice was sweet and childlike.

He had to think fast. He peered in front of him and saw a white skirt standing just in front of his hiding spot. He couldn't think of anything to say, so he went with whatever came first. "Stay back, little girl," he choked. "I'm contagious. You don't want to get sick."

Her skirt shuffled as she shifted her feet. If he could see her, he would have seen a hand rise to her hip and her eyes roll. "No, you're not. The Plague hasn't existed for centuries. Also, I'm not a little girl. Come on out."

He remained silent, unsure of what to do. He watched the bottom of her frilly skirt, anxiously waiting for it to disappear out of sight, but it never moved. She spoke again, this time her voice clear, but sympathetic. "I'm not going to tell on you, if that's what you're afraid of. Will you please come out and say hi?"

Ben panicked stammered out more excuses. "Uh, eh - I'm the only existing case of the plague. I swear it. Uh...now go home or you'll get sick."

He could hear her sigh in exasperation. She wasn't buy it at all.

"Well, even if that's true, Plague Boy, I thought the guy in the weird coat and top hat said you couldn't talk."

"Yeah. Well, I can." *Brilliant.*

Ben saw the skirt fold underneath her knees as she knelt down to look at him. She reached her hand out as if gesturing to a scared puppy. He scurried further under the wagon like a cockroach, sliding down onto his belly and hiding his face. He desperately wanted to talk to her and tell her everything, but he knew that it would never be worth Ringmaster's rage. The show had to be close to ending and he knew he was fucked if she didn't leave soon.

She continued to coo at him. "Come on out, Plague Boy. He is still doing his act, okay? He's got two more to go before the show is over, I swear. Now come on out before I drag you out."

He didn't know how she knew there were only two

more acts, but the thought flitted away in his nervousness. His heart quickened as he poked his head out in defeat, looking up at a loose skirt and tight bodice hugging the thin frame of a woman. He finally saw her beautiful and cherub face framed with bouncy, blonde curls falling over blushed cheeks. She was so tiny, built like a doll. *Women never have their hair down in public like that*, he thought to himself. He liked it, though. He wanted to flourish and tell his life story to her, everything he could pour out. Instead, he blurted. "Hi."

She smiled. "Hello."

"Why are you here?"

"Uh, because I like carnivals?"

"Oh."

After a few awkward moments of silence, he slid his entire body out from under the wagon and stood up next to her. She was about the same height as him, but delicate and slender. He looked off to the side as he said, "Well, I guess I meant why are you here talking to me? What did you want?"

Her eyes lowered and she smiled flirtatiously. "You're interesting and different. I figured you would have some good stories for me. Is that a good enough reason? It gets so boring here in Kentucky."

Not even close to New York, he thought. "Well, what did you want to talk about?"

"I don't know. What's it like working as a freak for that weird Ringmaster Tom?"

He was caught off guard by her strange and specific question. "Uh, fine. It's fine. You get to travel a lot. People look at you. Sometimes they point and laugh, other times they get scared. It's fine."

"I wouldn't think that's fine. I would hate that."

Ben shrugged and scratched at the mole on his face. He wished that just for the minute he could be normal looking for her. She stared curiously at the gigantic mole and her eyebrows raised. "Does that hurt?" she asked.

"What?"

"The thing on your face." She paused. "Well, the things on your body. Does it hurt at all?"

He looked down at his spotted arms. The bumps and scars were like hairy polka dots. "No. It doesn't feel like anything. Just...skin."

"So you don't have the plague then."

"No. Just looks like it."

She nodded and looked him up and down. He was used to being stared at, but she made him feel so uncomfortable and self conscious. He shifted on his feet.

"What is your name? Don't tell me it's Bubonic Boy either."

"Ben."

"Okay, Ben. I'm Beatrice."

"Okay."

He stared down, far away from her pretty face. He wished he knew how to talk to women. She must have felt his uncomfortable shyness because she giggled. "Look, I can leave. Just thought you'd enjoy a conversation tonight. Must get boring not being able to talk to anyone besides the freaks. If you ever want to chat, I'll be in town. I'd like to know more about you and maybe some stuff about that guy you work for."

"Why? He's kind of old for you, isn't he?"

She blushed and Ben knew he said the wrong thing. *God, I'm terrible at this.*

"No, not like that, you dummy. I mean I want to find out more about what he does. Maybe I'll ask him myself later since you're so scared."

She turned to leave and from some unknown burst of desperation, he quickly grabbed her wrist. She stared down at the spotted hand as he gathered up what little courage he had and said, "Please understand that I want to talk to you, Beatrice, but I will be in big trouble if I get caught. I'm sorry."

"If you're that scared, you should just run away. I'd rather be alone than living like you."

She smiled sadly at him, then shook her wrist free and walked back to the carnival, her white skirt bouncing across the grass. Ben wanted to call her back, tell her anything she wanted to hear, but he heard a round of cheers from beyond the stage and then a hard knock on the wooden side of the wagon. The show was over and Ringmaster would be back any minute. He ran over to the opening in the wagon canvas and slipped inside.

CHAPTER 4

The rest of the shows for the night didn't have the same pull as the first one. A lot of the crowds were the same folk from the previous viewings, which was common for small town carnivals. Not a lot of people lived in the area and they only got one night to go out and have a little fun away from work. They'd stay until the park closed for the sake of forgetting their real lives, if only for a few hours.

Fans of freak shows varied from state to state. Some towns couldn't get enough of them and others would burn their stage down if they weren't so afraid of God's watchful eye. This town was so-so with a few rounds of cheers and a couple laughs, but nothing remarkable. Everyone in the Brigade seemed accustomed to it except for Ringmaster, who somehow always expected a city crowd out of poor town folk. Whenever the shows did poorly, he would drink, and heavily at that. Then again, whenever they had an exceptional show, he'd have a celebratory drink, too. He basically drank whenever he could. Somehow he always had a bottle that magically appeared in his hands and nobody ever knew where they came from. For Ben, Ringmaster's drinking could either be a blessing or a burden, depending on how much money he made that night. If it was a good night, he was at least cheerful and kept the whip stowed for another day. If it was a bad night, the Freaks knew to hide and stay out of his way.

Ben drifted off to sleep quickly after they finished the last show for the night. He was hardly back in the wagon and still removing his mask as he curled up and passed out on his thick, itchy blanket. It may have belong to a horse at some point in time, judging by the smell, but anything that was soft was welcome relief from the heavy overcoat. The adrenaline of almost being caught talking to Beatrice had worn him out and stole away his energy for the last few shows. He figured it would be a peaceful sleep since Ringmaster didn't seem too agitated tonight. He closed his eyes and sighed heavily, waiting for sleep to come.

A heavy boot dropped down on his chest and pressed heavily against him. Before he could startle awake to catch his breath, he heard the familiar Ringmaster growl. "I'm not happy with what I saw tonight, kid. Not happy at all."

Ben's eyes snapped open to see Ringmaster standing above him, whip in one hand and whiskey bottle in the other. A lantern was set down next to the blanket, outlining the drunken man in shadows. He was a large, round silhouette, shadows of hair blazing from his head like wildfire.

Ben stared silently, knowing better than to speak. He was far too familiar with the game that Ringmaster liked to play. He lay patiently and, knowing not to look Ringmaster in the eyes, stared at the tip of the boot pointing at his chin. Waiting was the only way to get out of this kind of situation with the least amount of pain.

Ringmaster spoke slowly, although his first few words slurred together lazily. "First show tonight. Do you remember what happened?"

Ben continued to wait.

"No? Don't want to answer me, do ya boy? Well, let me tell you what happened, then. I heard you whisper to that midget to get you off stage. Your mask is, oh, what did you say? 'Hot as hell?' Let me explain something to you."

Ringmaster paused to take a swig from his quickly emptying whiskey bottle. Ben continued to stare at the boot, but grimaced in fear.

"If I can hear you talking past the stage, the whole audience can. If the whole audience can hear you, that means that you're not quite as sick as they thought and the entire fucking illusion is dead on its feet. Do you understand how risky that was?"

The boot pressed harder into Ben's chest. He gagged and put his hands up to pry the weight off of him, but the pressure continued to build. Ringmaster took a swig from his bottle, grunted, and continued. "I saved you from certain death and you repay me by embarrassing me in front of everyone? What do you have to say, kid? Speak up!"

Ben swallowed and picked his words carefully and slowly, knowing it was now his turn in this delicate position. "I would never embarrass you or bring shame to this show, Ringmaster, sir. What I did was wrong and I deserve a beating for it. I will not deny my wrongdoing and I beg your forgiveness. But know that it will never happen again."

As Ringmaster continued to glare down his chest, Ben started to writhe in pain. The weight was building on him. His body felt like it was going to cave. The bottle waved in circular motions dramatically above Ben's head, spilling whiskey like raindrops. "Oh, it will never happen again? How lucky am I! All worries are for naught because this fucking freak here says it will never happen again."

He lifted his boot from Ben's chest and poised to kick

him. Ben squeezed himself into a ball and put his hands up over his face, waiting for the familiar kick to the stomach. He clenched his eyes shut and whimpered. He heard Ringmaster mutter under his breath and felt more drops of whiskey trickle on his head. When the blow never came, he opened his eyes.

Ringmaster lost his balance, stumbling back and forth as he tried to regain his posture. His feet slipped from under him and he dropped into a pile of props and costumes with a loud crash. Ben wanted to laugh at the sight of it all, but knew he couldn't press his luck anymore. Instead, he crawled over to the debris of props and lifted Ringmaster from the now ruined Werewolf cage. His heart sank as he glanced over the broken bars and wooden scraps that used to be the main prop for the show "Oh shit," stammered Ben. "Oh shit. You've got to be kidding."

He put Ringmaster's limp body aside and picked up the wooden pieces, holding them together as if they would simply snap back into place. "You're going to blame this on me, I know it. Ringmaster, are you alright?

The body shook in a violent cackle. "Alright? Well, I'm just great kid," Ringmaster slurred sleepily. "They're going to take my show away and there's not a whole lot I can do about it, those fuckin...." he murmured a few unintelligible words and drifted off into a heavy sleep.

As Ben shook his head and stared at the rubble, unaware of what his next step should be, Trot peeked his head up quickly from a corner and looked down at Ringmaster's unconscious body. Not long after, Hot's appeared as well. Ben stared at them and Trot shrugged. Hot and Trot somehow always knew when it was the right time to disappear. They had years on Ben and were small enough to fit in the best hiding spots. "What the hell, you two! You were here the whole time? Why didn't you help me?"

Hot ignored the question. "What did he just say?"

Ben shook his head. "I have no idea. Something about someone taking his show away and then he fell asleep. It doesn't matter, it doesn't mean anything. He's drunk again."

Hot looked at Trot. "He's been drunk a lot lately, huh?"

"He's always drunk" Trot replied.

"No, I mean more than usual. I wonder what's been going on."

Ben ran a hand through his hair as he stared at the unconscious man. "You guys are going to back me up if he wakes up and forgets he broke this cage, right?"

Trot lowered his head again silently and disappeared out of sight. Hot shuffled under the blanket and closed her eyes, suddenly asleep.

"Damnit," Ben muttered.

He didn't want Ringmaster to wake up and see the damage done, nor try to recollect exactly what happened. Grabbing the man by the bottom of his slacks, he pulled him towards the lip of the wagon. With a quick tug, the body slumped out and hit the ground in a thump. Dust rose in sheets around him. Ben winced in fear and peered through the dust, waiting to hear the wrath conjure up from the drunken man, but he never stirred.

It was only about a hundred feet before his arms grew tired from dragging Ringmaster's dead weight. He didn't think he could make it all the way back to his wagon and tuck the man in like it never happened. He was far too heavy for that kind of work. Ben looked up at the clear sky and assumed it should be fine to leave him outside. As he dusted off Ringmaster's vest and pants and straightened his hair, he wondered what exactly he would say. He had dealt with this on several occasions, but never before were any of Ringmaster's prized possessions thrown into the mix. He knew he would just have to sleep on it and hope he had a good answer by morning.

After Ben looked over his work and was satisfied with how Ringmaster cleaned up, he stepped back inside the wagon and took to a corner, laying down and eying the broken cage. He thought about how these outbursts were starting to become routine. Ringmaster's drinking had been much heavier than usual and he stored bottles all over his wagon, reaching for them whenever a show was over. He had talked to Commodore about it a few days before. "The beatings are getting more severe," Commodore had said as he nursed an open cut on his arm from the whip. "What did we do that's so wrong? Why does he get so angry?"

Ben had shook his head and said, "You think your arm is bad? I ripped my overcoat one night on a loose nail from the shitty stage. I asked Ringmaster to mend it for me and he smashed a bottle right into my nose and said 'I'm not your whore!' You remember that?"

Commodore nodded and sighed. "Rule one of the Brigade: Never ask Ringmaster for anything. If he wanted to give it to you, he would have already done it." He ripped a scrap of a shirt and wrapped it around his flabby arm. "Maybe one day he'll cheer up and realize it's not so bad. He'll see that we're trying our best out there."

Ben slapped Commodore on the back and smiled at him, knowing deep down that was never going to be the case.

As the thought ended, he was suddenly tired again and desperately wanting sleep. He curled up onto the floor as comfortably as he could and instead started to think about the pretty girl he met tonight. Her skirt was so white and clean, even in the dusty fairground dirt. Her hair fell in soft yellow ringlets across the front of her blouse. He thought about how she'd look with her blouse unbuttoned a bit at the top and her skirt hitched a little higher and her mouth that probably tasted like fairy floss...

"Ben!"

He jumped as Trot poked his head out from the corner again. "What? Trot, you scared me."

"What are you doing?"

"I'm - I'm just thinking. What do you want?"

"I did some thinking, too. I'll second your story if he forgot he broke the fucking thing." Trot smirked. "Not like you need another whipping, right? Goodnight, kid."

Ben returned the smirk and nodded. He rested his head back down and this time fell right to sleep, unable to think of any excuses until morning.

CHAPTER 5

Beatrice sat on a bale of hay, kicking her feet and playing with a handful of pebbles, bouncing them and shaking them like dice in her tiny hand. Beside her, Ringmaster's unconscious body lay motionless. She lobbed the tiny stones at him, one by one, trying to land one in his open mouth. They bounced off his fat cheeks and nose. "You need to lay off the alcohol, Tom," she said. "It'll kill you."

His body did not stir. She sighed and threw the rest of the handful at him, pebbles bouncing everywhere around him. "I can't be wasting my time like this. I've got a lot of people to see tonight and you holding me up is not helping your case right now."

She stood up and hiked up her skirt a bit to step over his chest and straddle him. She leaned down, bringing herself face-to-face. As she moved in, she was quickly overwhelmed by the stench of his sour whiskey breath that heaved out of his body like toxic fumes. She plucked one of his eyelids open and saw a rolled back eyeball.

"TOM."

The eye didn't move.

"Now you're really testing me, you know that?" She reached down the front of her blouse and pulled out a small vial filled with a strange, bubbling liquid. She removed the lid and placed it just under Ringmaster's nostrils, waving it back and forth. Instantly, his eyes bulged open and he sat up violently, almost knocking her off her feet. He coughed and rubbed at his nose as she remained crouched over him.

"Tom. We need to talk."

Ringmaster stared at her, his brain still not caught up to his now alert body. "What?"

"Do you recognize me?"

He blinked several times to bring her into focus, but his head was pounding and everything was blurry. All he could make out was blonde ringlets and a white dress, so he took a stab in the dark. "Uh, yes. Yes I do. The girl with the dove! Hello, miss. Yes. Uh...what brings you here?"

She smirked at him and placed her hands on his temples, bringing his face up to hers. "Look deeper, friend. You're not that attractive for a young girl to be hanging around, as much as you'd like to think. Who else could I possibly be?"

He gazed at her, confused and uncertain, until he saw a familiar red fire burning behind otherwise blue eyes. He sighed heavily, his head sinking into his shoulders. "Yes. I think I got it. So, tell me, what name are you going by today?"

"Beatrice. Bee for short, if you'd like."

"Bee. Clever." His voice was flat and defeated.

She reached her arm behind her back as she smiled wickedly at him. "I've got a surprise for you that I thought you might like."

She brought the hand forward and in it was the dove he had released for her, only now it was singed and burnt into a crispy, black pile of ash. Tom stared at it in horror and she laughed softly to herself. "How do you do that trick anyway, Tom?"

He rubbed at his forehead, staring at the charred remains piled in her palm. He could see a few bird bones mixed in the ashes. "They're just white pigeons. Keep one in the pocket and hope it's not dead before you get to release it."

"Simple, but very neat. I was impressed."

Beatrice smiled and tossed the bird over her shoulder as she stood up. She reached a small hand out to Ringmaster, who took it reluctantly and pulled himself up. He stumbled forward drunkenly, but Beatrice's tiny body held his weight up with no problem. She was incredibly strong for her size.

"So, how has our deal been coming along? Anything to report to me?"

He shrugged and looked at the ground, composing himself as carefully as he could. He knew he had a lot of bullshitting to do and had to step carefully around his own lies. "I've been in a bit of a pinch these days. The freak show audiences aren't so good anymore. You saw it tonight - hardly a handful of people. No crowd, no Throwaways."

She laughed at him. "Really? Cut the crap, Tom. I may be little right now but that doesn't change what I can do to you."

She stepped a tiny step forward, which was enough to send Tom stumbling back in fear. His head nodded up and down frantically as he clung to a bale of hay to steady himself. "I know, I know. Believe me, you don't have to tell me twice."

Swallowing hard, he tried to think of more excuses as he lies poured from his mouth. "The truth is, the Throwaways have been taking off before I can get to them. I can't just do it as soon as I sign them, you know? It would be suspicious."

He turned away from Beatrice and started to brush

off his dusty pants. "They're not as easy to trick these days as they used to be." He muttered under his breath, "Not like the dozens I've given you through all these years."

Her head cocked in disbelief. "Oh, sure. That makes sense. It just seems strange to me that you haven't collected one in about, what, two months? They're all just so clever and cunning that they get out of Ringmaster Tom's clutch? Come on. Do you expect me to believe that the woman with no legs is going to run out of town on you tonight?"

"If she does, then I'll just get a different one next week," he retorted anxiously. "You know, for someone who was supposed to keep me in the business, you sure have been giving me some awful crowds lately. How can I hold up my end of the deal if you don't hold up yours?"

Before he could regret his poor choice of words, she was already on him. Ringmaster felt a burning hand on his neck begin to squeeze. He gasped for breath, the grip strong enough to crush bone. Her voice was deeper, coarser now. "Stop lying. Tell me what's going on. I give you new chances every week and I keep the police from meddling in our affair. I've given you the easiest job out of all the soldiers. Everything is in line for you to have your silly little show and all the fun you want. All you have to do is collect for us. The deal was that you get to keep the show and you give me the Throwaways." Her grip tightened and he violently lurched. "We have been very patient with you and it's starting to wear thin."

Tears collected in his eyes and he whispered, "I can't kill anymore."

She loosened her fingers and stared at him, burning. "Why?"

"It's getting so hard to do now. I'm an old man and

I've paid my dues."

She squinted her eyes at him, unsure of whether or not this was yet another lie. "You're getting soft on me."

"I'm not," he begged. "It's not the blood or struggle or any of that. I'm just getting tired of this deal."

"No, I think you're becoming sympathetic."

He lowered his eyes from hers. "Maybe I am. Sometimes I wonder if some of them were decent people. It's not their fault that they're disfigured or strange. Maybe they don't deserve to die and I'm wrong about this whole thing."

Beatrice pulled her hand back and, once free, he rubbed at the burning spot on his neck. She tsked softly through her teeth as she watched him. Her voice suddenly became soft and sweet again, like the tone when she spoke to Ben. "How noble of you, but so misinformed. Why do you think they appear the way they do? Why are children born without legs or mangled beyond repair? Aren't they but God's rejects? Why would God, a being supposedly so wrapped up in goodness and purity, make such abominations? They're nothing but tortured and fallen angels, Tom. They're ours because they belong with us. God didn't want them, just the same way he didn't want us. All we are asking of you is to collect them and pass them to us so we can put them where they belong."

Tom shook his head stubbornly like a child. "But why is this still my job to collect? I don't want to be a soldier anymore. I was promised that I could move up the ranks, but that was over forty years ago! I'm still at the bottom rung with not much mortal life left to live! Haven't I earned my keep?"

Beatrice's eyes flickered as the anger began to grow again. "Earned your keep? You've given us nothing! We let you have your show and your second-rate fame and all we want in return is what we bargained for. How exactly have you earned your keep?"

He lowered his head silently as he realized he had no argument. A deal was a deal and it didn't matter if he wanted to keep his end of it or not, he simply had to. Who was he to argue with her? When she was satisfied with his defeated silence, she lowered her voice to almost a whisper. "Tom, we need to see bodies and we need them now more than ever. If we are ever to build our Brigade for the War, you know what must be done. If you're having moral dilemma over this, clearly you're on the wrong side of it."

She turned her back to walk away. "Go seek Michael and see if he'll take you."

Tom raised his head and stood up straight like a soldier, feigning his enthusiasm that he once held years ago. "No. I serve only you and the Master."

She nodded slowly in approval. "If you give us the work that you provided us with thirty years ago, we will discuss your mortality then. Who knows? I may need you by my side when we finally reign again, but only if you stop lying to me. Is that clear?"

He hardly believed her, but he knew the argument was already over. "Understood."

"Good!" Beatrice gave Tom a sharp slap on the back, stinging and making him wince. "Oh, and by the way. Keep an eye on the plague boy. "

"What?"

"He covered for you quite well. Wouldn't say much to me. Either you trained him to keep his mouth shut or he's just stupid, but he's going to be quite the handful if you don't keep him in line."

Ringmaster's face swelled with rage. "He spoke to you? He is supposed to go immediately in the wagon after every show!"

She shrugged as she paced around, kicking pebbles and clumps of grass. "I don't know why you picked him to keep. I've seen the real Plague and he does not have the look...."

He ignored her as he continued to complain. "That son of a bitch...how many times do I have to tell him? You know, he almost ruined my show tonight, too. He had the nerve to talk during one of the performances and anyone could have heard him. I bet even you could have! That son of a bitch, I should just give him to you right now."

Beatrice shook her head. "Although I like your enthusiasm, I would rather take the fat one off your hands. He'd be an excellent Glutton trophy for the Boss."

Ringmaster's eyes widened. "What? I can't give you The Commodore! He's one of my best freaks. I've had people come several nights in a row just to see him!" How do you expect me to keep my show alive and collecting Throwaways if I don't have a solid stage act?"

Beatrice shrugged again and said, "Don't press your luck any further, Tom. You're on thin ice and we're underneath it when it breaks."

Beatrice stared at him, fire smoking and burning behind soulless eyes. Tom felt it radiating deep within him, stirring an old, familiar fear. Whenever she was on the tipping point, he knew one wrong word could end in horrible consequence. "When do you want him, then?"

"I think by Monday is not too much to ask of you. Make it happen and then we can talk about the status of your current debts. Thanks, friend."

Before he could make any retort, he realized she was already walking away, skirt bouncing behind her with every step. Tom watched until she was nothing but a dark speck past the trees and he realized he needed another drink.

CHAPTER 6

The next morning Ben woke up from a thin sleep, still drowsy and already wishing he could turn over and go right back to it. Instead, he stood up and stretched his arms and legs out, blankly looking at the remnants of the broken cage. His brain slowly started to piece it together, kicking in motion and recollecting the night. He blinked. "Oh shit," he muttered. "Hot. Trot. Ya here, guys?"

He looked over to the opposite corner of the wagon and saw the two of them sleeping together side by side, wrapped in tiny blankets. He stumbled over and knelt beside them, gently pushing and shaking them. The only response was a soft snore from Hot, so Ben shook harder. "Guys," he pleaded. "Please, wake up. We've got to find Ringmaster and tell him about the broken cage."

Trot mumbled an obscenity at him and turned over sleepily.

"Hey, wake up! You guys promised that you would defend me."

When they refused to stir, Ben sighed in disbelief and then slipped out of the wagon, ready to deal with Ringmaster. He stepped into his shoes and stumbled on the dry grass, each step a loud crunch. He felt his stomach tighten after every step, waiting for Ringmaster to rear his head with a bottle of whiskey and that whip he loved to carry around. He realized that he didn't even know what time it was when he woke. "Maybe he's still asleep," he told himself, trying to calm his already thing nerves.

If he was still sleeping in the grass, there would be time to carefully plan the story out and explain it rationally. If he was already awake, then there was nothing to do but accept the punishment. It was always the same when something turned up broken from one of Ringmaster's drunken nights - the blame would be on the first person he remembered from the episode, and that was going to be Ben. He scratched at one of the larger boils on his stomach as he nervously panned the grounds.

As his eyes darted back and forth, he saw a large, colorful blob out by the corner of the woods where the carnival grounds ended. It was Ringmaster, still fast asleep with his coat thrown over himself for a blanket. Ben's walk became slower and deliberate as he softly padded towards him to commence the battle he already lost. As he carefully approached, he began to think, *How did Ringmaster wind up all the way over by the trees when he was dragged beside the wagons. Maybe he got up and couldn't make it back?*

Ben knew it didn't matter and the thought quickly dropped from his mind as he approached the passed out old man.

Ringmaster's gut protruded from his undershirt, his hairy belly rising and falling with each heavy breath. His slacks were crumpled and dirty from sleeping in the dust. Next to him was an empty bottle. *I've never seen a man drink like he does,* Ben thought as he sat down beside the unconscious body and began to shake his arm.

Each snort and grunt in his sleep was another panicked twang in Ben's heart as he realized that he was definitely going to get beaten for the whole ordeal. "Ringmaster. Sir. Please wake up. We need to discuss something."

Ringmaster stirred and groaned, covering his eyes with his hands. "Boy, you better have a good reason to wake me up right now."

"I do sir."

Ringmaster uncovered one of his eyes and squinted at Ben. "Out with it, then."

"Last night Werewolf's cage broke."

"And how did that happen, boy?"

Ben swallowed. "Well, the honest truth? You came in drunk and told me someone was going to take the show away. Then you stumbled and fell into the cage. Sir, I wanted to fix it but I'm not really good at that sort of thing and I know it was an honest accident but I just wanted you to know-"

"Enough." Ringmaster sat forward, grunting and holding his head, trying to curb the dizziness. "Don't worry about it right now. We'll figure out something."

Ben nodded, waiting for the punchline like maybe a knock across the head. This was usually when Ringmaster cracked him with a fist or his whip. Instead, he stood up and started to hobble towards his wagon. Although it went against his logic, Ben asked carefully, "Are you okay, sir?"

Ringmaster huffed and said, "Yeah, never been better. Look, go get the others and eat your breakfast quickly. I'll be over there soon. I need to sit down and talk with you."

Ben nodded again and took off quickly before he could find out if this was some kind of set up. He dashed around the side of the wagon and knocked on the wood paneling, stirring the others. *Either he is planning some serious revenge for that cage, or something is wrong,* he thought to himself as he knocked.

CHAPTER 7

The Boss sat in front of her on a gigantic throne made of human flesh and cartilage. The structure of the chair was made of hundreds of femur bones, fused together with clumps of matted hair and blood. He himself was covered in gore, as well. His long, pointed fingers were forever stained orange from the blood he bathed in. Fresh pours of it splotched across his bare chest and mouth, running down to his thighs. He clenched a human skull between two of his fingers, rolling it back and forth like a marble.

He towered above her in her current form, easily two times the size of her tiny little body. Behind him stood jagged cliffs and never ending valleys consumed with fire and smoke. They were high above the action below, where cries of torture echoed up to him like a symphony hall. The smell of burning flesh and black smoke from the river below seemed to circle him like a horrific halo. He had the best seat in the house, but he was the Boss after all.

He looked down at her and she bent over into a formal bow. "Did you talk to your man?" he asked. The voice was loud and booming, thundering down to her.

"Yes, my liege."

"And what is the ruling?"

"Well, he's useless."

He leaned forward in his throne, bones crackling around him. "What do you plan to do about it, then?"

"Find another to take his place, my liege."

They paused to listen to the sound of ripping flesh and dry, raspy screams. He flicked the human skull down towards her and it caught on the hem of her white dress. She jumped aside and glared up at him "You've disappointed me this time," he said. "How am I to build an army if your men cannot even supply me simple souls?"

She said nothing and continued to stare, thinking about how much she hated Tom and how much she wished he was standing there in the firing line instead of her. The Boss continued to speak when he saw she had no response. "The next one will be better. Choose him wisely and that is your only warning. Do not come back until you are sure. Understood?"

"Yes, my liege. Thank you for this opportunity, my liege."

He motioned a powerful hand upwards, finger pointing crookedly at the earth ceiling above them. "Go."

CHAPTER 8

Ben opened the flap to the wagon and saw the freaks inside, devouring beans and coffee quickly. "Well, looks like everyone is up," he said as he pulled himself up inside the cramped space.

Commodore chewed loudly, beans spilling over his chin and neck. He had a towel on for a bib that he dabbed across his mouth, but it was hardly worth the effort, for he continued to spill more food on himself. Werewolf sat beside him, cup of black coffee cradled in his furry hands. He stared down into the murky water, tired and quiet. Ben patted him on the back in a friendly greeting and Werewolf responded with a small nod. "You okay, buddy?" Ben asked.

He shrugged a small shrug and Ben deciphered it. "Yeah, just tired? I know the feeling. I had a hell of a night, myself."

Commodore stopped chewing and licked at his lips as he asked, "The cage, right?"

Ben was reaching for a coffee cup and stopped dead in his tracks. "What? How did you know about that?"

Behind Commodore sat Hot and Trot, staring at the floor. Ben scrunched his face at them and smirked in disbelief at their hastiness. He stared at them as he continued to get himself a cup of coffee and said, "Huh, well look who is up bright and early in the morning. You know, it's funny that when I needed you to be awake to vouch for me that you're practically comatose, but the food comes out and suddenly you two are up and running."

Trot took a spoonful of beans and smacked his lips, chewing loudly to drown out the sound of Ben's voice, and Hot shrugged sympathetically. "We were scared, honey. I'm sorry about that, but we didn't know how the situation would play out. Did he talk to you about it?"

"Here's the weird thing. I told him about it truthfully, that he broke it and everything, and he didn't seem to care. He wants all of us to sit down and talk with him about something. I don't know what's going on."

Werewolf shrugged again, but this time he seemed more animated. His eyes moved up from his cup of coffee to Ben. He looked concerned and fearful. Ben smiled at him and said, "Don't worry about it. I'm sure we're fine. I mean, we bring in the best crowds, he has said it himself. It would be suicide to lose us now! He isn't letting any of us go, at least I don't think."

Commodore nodded his head, licking a bean off the corner of his mouth. "It's true. We've been doing great this year. You've got to have a fat guy and a werewolf and midgets, right? And Ben here brings in the money with the Bubonic act. There's nothing to worry about. Probably just going to tell us we have to add another show on to the night or something."

Everyone murmured in agreement except for Trot. He squinted his eyes and scratched his head inquisitively as he said, "But what about all the drinking lately? He's been pissed every night this week. I don't even know where he's getting all these bottles from!"

The flap snapped open and sunlight poured into the dark, dingy wagon. At the opening stood Ringmaster, fist gripping the wagon flap as he peered at Trot and grimaced. "You're lucky I've got bigger fish to fry," he said. "So, for the sake of time, I'm just going to pretend I didn't hear that."

Trot's eyes widened and he sat silent and attentive, his body slinking down into itself to hide away from the death glare. Ringmaster's eyes fell from Trot and met with The Commodore, who continued to shove beans into his face and chew loudly. Commodore smiled at him and no smile was returned back. Ringmaster cleared his throat and said, "Come outside and sit down, all of you. I want to talk to you and it's disgusting in here."

They all glanced back and forth at each other, hesitant and uncomfortable. Ben shifted in his seat and nudged at Werewolf, who shrugged in return. Ringmaster's fist gripped the wagon flap tighter as he barked, "What's the meaning of this? I said move!"

They remained silent for a few more moments until Trot built up the courage to speak. "But you say never to leave the wagon during the day," he said weakly.

Ringmaster's face turned red and he rapped his fist against the wooden panels. They jumped from the loud snap against the wood. "Get the fuck out!" He screamed, a large vein bulging in his neck.

He threw the flap back down, returning them to the darkness of the wagon. Ben squinted his eyes in the dark, now blind from the sudden adjustment. "Well," he mumbled. "You heard him. Let's go guys."

This time, without hesitation, they quickly piled out of the wagon one by one and sat down. Commodore was the only one who remained in the wagon, shimmying to the front and watching through the flap. The wood creaked and leaned as as his legs flopped down off the side and hung like giant slabs of meat. Ringmaster stared at the fat man and scratched at his frizzy hair. "I can't believe it," he snickered.

"Have you actually gained more weight? You're disgusting."

Commodore shook off the insult and simply smiled. "I'm working on my figure. Got to look good for the ladies we meet."

The other freaks chuckled, but Ringmaster shot a sharp look to them. "You think this is funny," he snapped, "but wait until you hear the news."

The smiles and laughter ceased quickly and they were surrounded by the agonizing silence of hot and windless summer air. Ringmaster raised his hands and looped his thumbs through his suspenders, eyes to the ground in thought. As he searched for the words to say to begin his speech, Ben watched him closely. Although Ringmaster was frowning, he could see in his eyes that the man was pleased about something. He knew whatever the news was, it was probably going to be another lie. Ben bit the inside of his cheek and waited patiently.

Pacing back and forth like a drill instructor, Ringmaster stepped in rhythm in front of the Brigade, "So, now that you're all not smiling anymore-" his eyes shot back to Commodore. He recoiled into the wagon slightly. "-We need to talk business. We've got a problem, Brigade. The money just isn't what it used to be. This year, there was a long winter into spring and it killed our finances. The crowds have been weaker and weaker, and the pay thinner. The expenses are just not worth it anymore, so I'm ending The Devil Brigade."

The freaks stirred, looking at each other in confusion and shock. Werewolf stood up and stared at Ringmaster, shrugging his shoulders dramatically. Commodore and Trot looked at each other in horror, and Hot was the first to speak up. She stood and put her hands on her hips. "This must be some kind of a joke," she said.

Ringmaster's cheeks swelled in anger. "Does this sound like a joke? Another remark like that and I'll kick you across the goddamned field. Sit down and shut up, all of you."

The shifting stopped and Werewolf and Hot sat down reluctantly. Ben continued to watch the situation, staring deep at the eyes of Ringmaster. There was a glint of pure happiness behind that anger, and that was what confused Ben the most. He knew firsthand that the winter was short and brisk. The crowds were as strong as they have always been, give or take a few nights. He knew exactly what was happening - the lies were huge.

Ringmaster began to pace again, this time faster as he spoke. "Now, listen to me. I can't afford this any longer. We used to bring in hundreds of spectators and a whole variety of crowds. Do you all remember that or are you too stubborn to admit it?"

He paused for debate. Everyone knew better than to actually take up an argument, so they sat in silence until he began again. "We're old news now," He said. "Every town has seen your act. The carnivals don't want to sign us anymore and I can't say that I blame them, what with how awful things have been."

Ringmaster turned on his heels and faced to the right. Ben noticed how old Ringmaster really was – his hair white and wiry and his face starting to sag. Jowls scooped down on his face and he no longer was the sharp man who first took him on board. Despite all the age, Ben saw a tiny smile on his lips as he said, "Tomorrow we're going to have to go our separate ways. I can't afford to buy you train tickets or send you off or anything sentimental like that.

You're just going to have it figure it out for yourselves. It's been a nice summer so far, so it shouldn't get too cold at night if you have to walk."

Ben sat and drank in the words, feeling the fear sink his heart. He looked around at the other freaks and saw similar faces of disbelief and sadness. Ben blurted out, "What are we going to do, sir? There's nowhere for us to go."

"That's not my problem," Ringmaster replied casually. "I've got myself to take care of and you're all adults here. Find another show that will tolerate your bullshit as much as I have."

Ringmaster laughed to himself and before Ben could pry any more, they heard the wagon behind them start to shake and creak. He and all the others turned to see Commodore, groaning and shaking the wagon frame as he slammed his fists against the panels violently. Each flailing of his arms shook the flimsy frame. "Tolerate our bullshit? Is that what you've been doing?"

Ringmaster folded his arms and peered at the man. "Do you have something you need to say to me, you pig?"

"We've done nothing to you," Commodore snarled. "We take the beatings and eat the slop and do everything you've ever asked of us. We break our asses to bring in crowds and you treat us like animals and act like this is *our* fault?"

Ben watched in horror as the gigantic man swung his arms down to the edge of the wagon and tried to lift himself up to stand. His flabby arms and legs quivered with the movement as he pushed his weight up off the wagon and set his bare feet down onto the ground. Holding himself up like a toddler, he wobbled on thick ankles, unable to let go of the wagon sides. Ben rose to stop him, but Werewolf grabbed his arm and gently pulled him back down, shrugging his shoulders sadly. Ben knew what Werewolf was telling him, so he sat and watched hopelessly.

Commodore removed his hands from the wagon and for a brief moment, was standing on his own. He lifted a heavy foot to start approaching Ringmaster, who watched with a wicked smile on his face. "Oh, really? You're going to come teach me a lesson, are you? Come on fat man. Come over here and show me what you've got."

His eyes filled with fear and pain as he lowered the foot down again in a giant, awkward step. Fruitlessly, pudgy arms flailed as they tried to regain balance to his massive frame. With a twist of a fragile ankle, he tumbled. As his belly hit the ground, he grunted and seemed to almost bounce. Ben's heart sank and he felt Werewolf's hand grip tighter.

Ringmaster heaved a raucous laugh, doubling over and pointing at Commodore laying helpless and squirming. "That's it? That's your fight? Well, you sure showed me, didn't you?"

Ben pushed Werewolf's hand off of him and stood, rushing over to Commodore to help sit him up. "Come on, Commodore. I've got you," he said softly as he rolled him onto his back as gently as he could. He then clasped his hands and lifted him forward, helping Commodore to sit upright. As he sat up, Ben could see the tears and flush cheeks. Ringmaster continued to cackle and hold his sides. "You alright, buddy?"

Ringmaster coughed on his laughter and wiped away a false tear. "Oh, that was good," he giggled. "So, what were you saying, fat man?"

Commodore's eyes grew wide with rage. "What kind of devil are you?" he whispered.

The laughter stopped and for a moment there was silence and stillness again. Ben wished it could just stay like that, this whole situation ended and all set back to normal. But the sudden stomping of Ringmaster's boots approaching made it clear that this was not over.

He marched up to the wagon, stepping over the others blindly, and knelt down in the grass, face to face with Commodore. His lips twisted into a sneer as he quietly, said, "I'm the kind of devil that's doing every one of you a favor that I don't have to. Don't ever talk to me like a fool. I have a reason for everything I do, so don't ever think I'm not one step ahead of you."

Commodore tightened his jaw and ground his teeth as he said, "What could possibly be worse than abandoning us to die?"

Ringmaster's upper lip curled into a sneer and his head began to shake back and forth in disbelief. "I ought to whip that rudeness right out of you, Commodore," he whispered.

His eyes never left Commodore's as he reached down to his belt to retrieve his whip, but before he could raise his arm back up, a thick fist swung down on his nose in a flash, blood spurting down to the collar of his shirt as the bridge of his nose snapped. Ringmaster stumbled backwards and pressed his hand up to his face, blood trickling through his fingers. He stared down at his hand as Commodore kept his fist up, ready for the fight to begin. Ben could see that the rage in Commodore had already subsided and now his fist was raised in fear and uncertainty.

Ringmaster stared at the blood that made ribbons

down his hand and onto his shirt sleeve. "You've made a mistake," he whispered. "You'll regret this."

He turned to the rest of them, his eyes burning, as he roared, "You'll all regret this!"

His finger pointed wildly at each freak one by one as he said, "I've given you everything you've ever needed and I'm trying to do you a service right now. I've been nothing but good to you, saving you from the inevitable, but obviously that isn't good enough for any one of you. The show is over after this weekend and that's all there is to it. I don't want to hear about this anymore, so I'll see you all tonight. I need to clean up and get ready for our final shows, and I suggest you do the same."

He covered his nose again, wincing as his finger brushed against the demolished bridge. He stomped past the Brigade and out an opening in the fence to the empty carnival, far away from the freaks before any more damage or argument could be had.

Ben looked over to Hot and Trot. They sat silently, staring at Commodore and his still raised fist. He could see that they wanted to get up and help, but they were too afraid to get involved. The silence thickened amongst them. Even Werewolf seemed uncomfortably quiet, neither shrugging nor grunting but rubbing his hands together in nervousness.

As Ben stood and approached the wagon, he saw Commodore's face was empty and fearful. He had no idea what he had done or that he had that kind of violence inside him. Ben could see it all in his widened eyes and sweaty forehead. He put a hand on the man's shoulder. "You alright?" he asked softly.

Commodore looked at his fist still held high above his head. "Uh, yeah," he said as he lowered it. "I think so.

Ringmaster deserved it. Right, guys?"

Everyone nodded, but didn't say a word. After they disbanded and went about their usual work and business for the rest of the afternoon, they did it silently and without the usual chat. There just didn't seem to be anything to talk about as the sun went down and the stage was built.

CHAPTER 9

Beatrice was sitting patiently on a wooden bench inside the carnival. The grounds were small in this town, only enough room for some simple ring toss games and a few stage acts that were easily packed up and sent to another town. One of the stages was brown and black with a western frontier saloon door attached to it. There were horse saddles and posts for when the Wild Wild West Show played out early in the evening. Small towns like these never got Buffalo Bill's traveling show, which was starting to take off in Europe. His show was full of excitement and fun, so they had to take what they could get with the knock off version. Next to the Wild West stage was a smaller, cheaper stage where the belly dancers would twist and gyrate to music and men would happily watch as they ate sweets.

Beatrice liked watching the small town shows herself. She liked to see the rush of excitement and sin shroud a town as the oddities and shows came through. Men could fantasize freely about the strange, exotic women who danced rhythmically in front of them. Meanwhile, as they hid erections and made kissy faces at the dancers, their wives could gossip and hiss about the other women in town, calling them blasphemers as they drank their fill of whiskey from hidden flasks. All of it made Beatrice happy. The big cities were full of deprivation and she was sure that she could build the Brigade from those kind of folk. When she saw evil spread across a small town though, she was always much more satisfied.

She sat on the bench and smiled as she thought about her work and tapped her finger on a chessboard in front of her. Small black and white beechwood pieces speckled the board in what appeared to be a random placement. She eyed the pieces one by one, pondering her next move. She was the best chess player she knew and liked to play by herself, her only worthy opponent.

She looked up at the sun to see it's placement. She knew he would be arriving in any second, so she brought her attention back to the board and didn't need to look back up to see Ringmaster walking towards her direction. She could feel his eyes upon her and the pause in his motion. There was hatred burning inside him and that made her smile even more.

He stomped over and sat down at the bench across from her, fists tightly curled on the table. She lifted her eyes and noticed one hand covered in blood. "Do you need some medical attention, Tom?" she giggled.

He didn't smile. She could hear his teeth grinding as he said, "Funny seeing you here, you bastard. Why don't you just leave me the fuck alone and go bother someone else? I'm not in the mood for this right now. You must have other deals to concern yourself with, right?"

Beatrice's eyebrows rose dramatically, but her eyes remained on the chessboard as she tapped a dainty pointer finger on the bench. "You approached me," she said. "I was just sitting here playing a nice game of chess and you came storming over. It's a beautiful day – can't a lady just enjoy herself in the sun?"

His fist tightened and his knuckles turned white. "Oh? Is that right? You just happened to fucking be here?"

She looked up at him with a tiny smirk on her lips. Ringmaster noticed her skin was no longer a glowing porcelain and was starting to become almost translucent like a goldfish, veins and red spots building on her tiny arms as she spoke. "Life's funny that way, Tom. Don't sweat the small stuff, though. I'm on vacation here. Say, want to play some Chess with me? We could bet on it, make it a little more interesting."

Ringmaster slapped the chessboard off the bench and grabbed Beatrice by her curly blonde hair, gripping her from the scalp. Her body gave no resistance and she dangled under his grip. She laughed in surprise. "Is that a no?" she asked.

"No, I don't want to play!" He screamed at her. "I want my title and I want my fucking rank and I want it now."

The hair suddenly ripped and felt loose in his hands. It tore off the girl's head like velcro as his arm snapped back. He yelped and threw the hair in surprise. In the air, he saw a curly wig with little drips of blood and peels of skin dangling from it. She had disappeared from under it. His neck snapped back and forth as he looked for her, eyes darting in panic. He knew that something bad was about to come.

He heard a twig snap behind him and he turned into an invisible swift punch to his stomach. He toppled over the bench, his legs squirming as he heaved in pain. As he flipped onto his back and clutched his torso, struggling to catch his breath he noticed that the sky above him was cloudless and beautiful. The thought numbed him until a throb of pain instantly pushed it out of his mind and he reeled around. His breathing staggered and he panicked, thinking maybe his lungs had collapsed from the hard blow. He heard a sweet, innocent giggle again. "Oh, stop it. You're such a baby," she said.

Beatrice reappeared next to him, placing the chessboard back down beside him. She began to reset her pieces calmly, placing each one in their respective spot. Her face was docile and relaxed, only now she was completely bald. Red and black pulsing veins crossed the top of her skull and temple like thick ribbons. Blood trickled down the side of her face and into her eyes. She blinked it out casually and tapped her finger again in thought, as if completely unaware of her horrific appearance. Tom turned to look at her and gasped."

"Stop with the gasping," she said sarcastically. "You're going to be just fine. I just needed to remind you of where exactly you stood. Until the entire deal is done, you are still mortal. Right?"

Ringmaster sighed and averted his attention from her disfigured skull to the sky above. "Yes."

She nodded, droplets of blood splattering against the chessboard. "Alright, then. Now, on to other matters. But first, can I have my wig back, please? I feel a little naked without it."

Ringmaster rolled off the bench and limped over to the wig. Clots of blood and flesh hung from it like sliced meat. He shuddered and picked it up with two fingers, holding it as far away as possible from himself until he returned to her. She positioned it over the black throbbing veins and shifted it around until it fell back into place like a puzzle piece. The veins and blood seemed to disappear and she once again was a striking young lady. As she fixed one of the frizzed curls, she said, "What was that meeting about?"

He froze. "What meeting?"

"That little meeting you just had? I'm not stupid, friend. I saw you were trying to skip town on me. You were going to let the weirdos go and then hit the road."

He remained silent and looked down at the chessboard. She hadn't made her first move yet.

" I found that pretty interesting, though," she continued. "You do know that I pretty much see everything, right?"

"Yeah, I've noticed."

"Okay, so what exactly was your plan there?" She moved a black pawn forward two spaces for her first move.

"I don't know. I'm desperate."

"Desperate. Hmm," she murmured. Her eyes locked onto him. She noticed he was staring at the black pawn. "Want to play? The offer is still on the table."

"No, I don't think I can deal with any more games. Thanks, though."

"Your loss, Tom."

His eyes began to trace her. He remembered how beautiful and radiant she looked only the night before. Now her skin was getting gray and damp, her eyes no longer shining, but burning. He shook his head and spoke quietly. "Look, I'm out of options. I don't know what to do."

Beatrice snorted to herself. "No ideas, huh? Hey, I've got one. Kill them and give them to me?"

She laughed raucously, echoing across the carnival ground. He groaned and shook his head. "No, please. Don't make me do this anymore. What if I start new? Give me a new appearance and job and let me send you soldiers another way. I just need a fresh start, is all. I can prove my worth to you, just not like this anymore."

Beatrice made a few more chess moves. White, black, white. She didn't answer him.

"What do I have to do, Beelzebub?"

She ignored him, her concentration on the board as she swiftly moved the pieces. Tom watched her hands move quickly and easily, touching each piece in thought before another move. She didn't seem to take any time to plan, though. Each chess piece danced around the board, as if she played the same moves every time. "I can't give you a new job. That comes with prestige, Tom. Prestige you never earned. Either one of two things can happen now. Either you give me the Brigade or - "

She paused. The queen was open and vulnerable. She looked surprised, as if she didn't expect the opening. Tom looked down at the chessboard, then back at her impatiently. "What? What is my second option?"

She smiled, her eyes lit and alert. "Your second option is to walk away from this deal."

He shot up from the bench, staring at her and searching her face for trickery, but she was nothing but a sincere smile. "What are you talking about? I can get out of this?

"Yeah, I think so," she said. Her words were slow, as if she wasn't even sure herself. "You know what? Sitting here with you, seeing you this desperate and listening to your tale has got me thinking I need to approach this differently. You did good work us and what's fair is fair."

His eyes widened. "What are you saying?"

"I'm saying that you're absolutely right, Tom. If you don't want to do this anymore, just say the word and you're free. Of course, if you consider being a heartless murderer at any point again, we won't be able to hide bodies anymore, but you don't seem to want that perk anymore these days.

"You've supplied us with many a body for the Devil Brigade. You've given us at least one hundred soldiers throughout the years, haven't you?"

He nodded wildly. "One hundred and forty two."

"Wow." She folded her arms and smiled at him. "I've decided to let you go, Tom. Go be a normal, naive human again if that's what you want."

Tom laughed to himself nervously, studying her face for signs of deceit. "Is this part of a game? Are you being serious right now?"

"Dead serious. You're free if you want. Just remember who helped you out, old friend."

With that, Beatrice moved a rook next to the queen. The board was closing. "We made a deal and you can't meet the supply. If you don't feel committed to the cause anymore, I can truly understand that."

Ringmaster smiled, extending a hand in a friendly shake. "Well, thank you for your understanding, Sir. I think that it's been many years in the making and my retirement is due."

Beatrice took his hand and shook it limply, a thin smile staining her lips. "However," she said, her voice becoming stern again, "You're still going to give me the fat one though. Consider it your final notice to Big Boss, yeah?"

Ringmaster unconsciously reached up to his nose and felt dried blood flake off. "That I can do with pleasure. After him I'm done though, right?"

"You'll never see me in this life again."

He nodded and headed back towards the wagons, an excited bounce in his step. Beatrice lowered her head back down to her chessboard. Only two moves remained.

There was no need to finish the game since she already knew what those plays were going to be. It was time for her appointment with the Boss and she couldn't be late.

CHAPTER 10

The man was out fishing again, now with a brand new pole at a different lake. It was his second day at this new location and, after hours of baiting and bobbing the line, he still had no bites. No matter what fishing technique he used from his advanced repertoire, the water always remained dead and silent.

He scratched his nose and waited patiently, watching the water with absolute focus. He didn't like the current down time he had, but he didn't despise it either. It just told him that he was one second closer to the end. Every moment that nothing happened meant that something was just around the bend. He was a firm believer in that and God had proven it over and over again.

He stretched his long and masculine legs out in front of him, slowly raising and lowering his foot to a song that played inside him: his heart beat. He tapped his pulse out on a rock, listening to the soothing slow rhythm. He loved that sound. It was steady and balanced just like him. That was his job, to instill the balance.

As he tapped and began to lose himself in the mantra of his rhythm, he felt the slight pull of the line and heard the tiny splash as it submerged. A vibration ran into the handle of his pole and he stopped tapping. A nibble.

He remained motionless and waited. Another vibration, another nibble. He closed his hand around the handle and braced himself. First catch in a long time, but he knew better to rush it. Patience was what he was made of, anyway.

CHAPTER 11

Ben sat in the old wagon by himself, feet up on the remnants of the Werewolf cage, coloring in some of his less prominent boils with ink. The afternoon was best spent alone after what had happened with Ringmaster and Commodore, leaving everyone uncomfortable and worried. Even if everyone did want to talk about it, Ben didn't. It upset him to think about the fight and the abandonment that was on the horizon. They could all say their goodbyes later, just before they go their separate ways and find work. *It's a big country*, he thought, *there has to be something out there for us.*

He circled the spot on his thigh with the ink and colored it until the harmless boil became a grotesque tumor popping sickly from his pale skin. He admired his work and realized how good he was getting at perfecting his act. *Maybe I can run off to a new show,* he thought as he smiled. *One where they feed you bread and soup and let you eat fairy floss sometimes.*

He pictured the sweet candy, stringy and colorful, wrapped around a long stick. He saw one of the billowing pieces caught in the wind and suddenly rest on Beatrice's pink lips as she pursed them around the stick.

No, he thought to himself. *I really shouldn't think of her like that. I won't see her again anyway...*

His imagination ignored him. He smiled at the wagon wall as he watched her head pull back and pieces of the candy hung off her tiny mouth. It turned in a cute, knowing smile and all he wanted to do was reach out and kiss the candy right off of her. Before he could picture it, her tongue flicked out and licked her top and bottom lips. Ben shivered at the thought and smirked. He pictured those tiny hands pressing against his chest and those sweet lips kissing his neck, her candy breath wafting around him. The porcelain face and beautiful blue eyes met with his and he put his hand on the back of her head, the blonde curls wrapping between his fingers. As he pulled her in, he closed his eyes and pursed his lips, ready to meet hers.

Everything feels so real, his brain announced. His imagination ignored it and he gladly accepted the indulgence....

The pressure of his hand against the curly hair felt so real and soft. He'd never felt something so beautiful. His fingers clutched the curls and his sense of urgency pushed her hard against him. As she quickly came in, his hand shifted and slipped downwards, still clenching the hair. His eyes opened and he saw the blonde wig hanging freely in his hand, blood dripping from the smooth inside and strips of pale flesh dangling.

"Ugh!"

Ben sat forward and snapped awake, staring at the walls of the empty wagon. His heart raced as he glanced around, looking for Beatrice and the disgusting wig. "Beatrice?", he called weakly. He knew she wasn't there, but she had felt and smelled so real. He could practically taste the cotton candy and her lips and feel that terrifying wig in his fingers. He looked down at his hand and flexed it to fade the phantom feelings away.

As he stared at his hand, he heard the canvas top flip

open. He looked up to see Ringmaster staring at him, a bright smile on his face. "Get ready for a memorable night, my boy! Let's give the crowd the best we've got. Tell the others to look sharp and be ready!"

With that, he dropped the flap and was gone. Ben blinked, staring at the vacant area and trying to piece the whole situation together. *Forget Beatrice,* he thought. *I can't even begin to imagine what Ringmaster has in mind if he's this excited.*

He shook his head to release the fantasy and looked down to his lap. Whatever erection he had before was long gone. He picked up the ink brush and continued to carefully trace raised skin on his leg with precision, slowly pushing Beatrice and her candy mouth out of his mind.

CHAPTER 12

"Step right up, ladies and gentlemen!" Ringmaster bellowed to the hot carnival air. "Come see the most grand of performances to grace this lovely town! Welcome to the Devil Brigade!"

He perched on the corner of the stage, pointing his cane across the open grass before him. The sky was heavy with clouds and threat of rain, so the carnival was empty except for a handful of the dedicated townsfolk from the night before.

Ringmaster didn't seem to notice the absenteeism of a crowd, though. He stood tall on the stage, his wild hair pointing in all directions beneath the long top hat. His vest and coat were clean and the rainbow colors of the fabric shone in the light of the lanterns surrounding him. He danced wildly back and forth on the edge of the stage, pointing and dramatically waving at the few people who passed him by. "Step right up, my good friends! You won't want to miss my show tonight!"

He slapped at the posters on the frames, the cane cracking loudly into the silent night. An audience started to build and watch cautiously, but it was thin with only a few dozen disappointed carnival goers. Ringmaster welcomed them with waves and bows and behind him, the heavy curtain shrouded Ben and the others.

They stood there with no placement or idea of what they were supposed to do. Ben poked an eye out of the curtain to see the several people standing at the stage. "Thank God for that," he whispered to Werewolf. "I'd rather not embarrass myself in front of a giant crowd."

Werewolf shrugged at him in confusion and stared at Ben, waiting for an answer. Ben glanced back at him and said, "He doesn't want us to do the usual gimmick. I guess we just have to wait for his cues when he reveals us. Right?"

Werewolf shrugged again as Hot nudged Ben on the hip, staring confusedly at the sight of a happy Ringmaster between the curtains. "Hey, Ben. Do you have any idea what is going on?"

Ben just put a finger to his lips. He didn't want to spoil Ringmaster's mood and deal with the repercussion of talking behind the curtain. He'd had enough drama since yesterday. Hot glanced over at Werewolf, who, once again, shrugged his shoulders, only this time more sympathetically, as if he understood that the show was going to be a disaster. In front of the curtain, Ringmaster's voice boomed. "Thank you for your appearance on this somewhat gloomy day," he bellowed. "Let's not waste one precious minute. Allow us to introduce - The Devil Brigade!"

Ringmaster stomped his foot and Hot and Trot took it as their cue to reveal the stage. Each of them grabbed a curtain at the center and heaved it away. The Brigade stood in the center of the stage, one by one in some kind of military line. Behind them was Commodore, sitting on his table prop and balancing himself with his hands on the sides of it. They stood awkwardly and stared at the crowd in silence.

The handful of people applauded thinly, just staring back at the freaks scattered about the stage. Ringmaster cleared his throat and stomped his foot again, raising an eyebrow at the Brigade. "Well, my pets. Show them what it is you do!"

They glanced at each other anxiously, then began to move about the stage awkwardly, acting out their individual performances side by side. They walked back and forth and paraded around the stage in an ugly procession, no music or words spoken. It became cramped very fast as they all tried to do their small bits and Ringmaster danced among them, waving his cane and speaking in high bravado. "Look at them!" he cried to the audience. "Look at the wonder and mystery that is The Devil Brigade! Behold their ugliness, their disgusting bodies, and their awful movement! They are truly the most hideous thing I've ever seen. What about you?"

The sound on the stage rose as Ben stomped on his feet. Hot and Trot held hands as they skipped. Werewolf gripped at his shirt and stuck out the weird silver tongue repeatedly, unsure of what else he could possibly do for his bit without his cage. As the strange commotion continued, The Commodore could only sit and look at the several people who looked back at him. He shrugged at them and shook his head. Hot whispered to Ben as they circled around the stomping Plague monster costume, "What the fuck is this mess?"

The audience was littered with a few unsure claps and applause, but Ringmaster seemed to be in a world where thousands screamed and begged for more entertainment. He heard the echo of cheers and joy as his voice grew in volume and his movements became more dramatic, heavy bows and quick prancing between the Brigade. Meanwhile,the main acts struggled and bumped into one another on stage, desperately trying to keep composure. They squeezed by the Commodore,who watched in silence. Ben realized he refused to do his bit.

Ringmaster kept a watchful eye over all them, scaring them into their most enthusiastic performances. Even Werewolf stamped and ran back and forth across the stage, gritting his teeth and swiping at the other freaks and the audience for a few cheers.

They danced for five minutes until Ringmaster raised his cane above his head and circled it like a conductor. They fumbled back into standing position and stared at him. "Enough! Bravo, children! Bravo! You've done your Master proud. Let's hear it for my Brigade, folks!"

The audience no longer clapped. They were unamused at this point, bored of the entire set. Several of them had walked away a few minutes prior, leaving only four or five viewers. "Close the curtains, my little ones," he shouted to Hot and Trot with a swirling gesture of the cane. They stepped to the corners of the stage and pulled the curtain closed as quickly as they could, staring at each other in disbelief.

The Brigade left the stage puzzled and tired and piled into the wagon without a word. They gathered in and looked at one another, silent and unsure of what to do. Ben knew that everyone was fearing a whipping. Ringmaster couldn't possibly have been happy with their performance, despite the grand display he put on for the few people in the audience. Ben wrung his hands until he heard Ringmaster's final thanks and bows to the carnival. They all remained silent as they listened to his heavy boots crunching in the grass and approach the wagon. Ben held his breath and waited for the screaming as the wagon canvas flipped open.

Ringmaster climbed in beside Ben and pulled a flask of whiskey from one of his vest pockets. He took a swig, grimaced, wiped his mouth, and presented a wide smile. "Excellent work, my pets! Excellent work indeed!"

He handed the flask to Ben and made a motion as if to say 'drink up.' Ben took a stiff shot of the harsh, brown liquid and coughed. It may have been whiskey, but it didn't matter because the stuff was rancid and sour like old moonshine. He nodded at Ringmaster, squinting his eyes at the horrid taste on his tongue. "No, my boy. Pass it around! Let's have a drink on me, yeah?"

Ben turned and passed it to Werewolf beside him, who in turn sent it over to Hot and Trot. By the time it reached Commodore, though, it was empty save for a few drops. Commodore looked to Ringmaster and saw he had been staring the entire time, smiling in his direction. He responded with a small, suspicious nod and said, "I don't drink, but thank you. So, tonight was the last performance?"

Ringmaster's smile broadened. "Yes! Tomorrow night you are all free to go and get far, far away from me!"

Everyone knew it was easier to not fight about it again, so they all nodded and painted similar smiles on their faces. "What will you do, sir?" asked Ben.

"Ah, I'm not sure yet. I've got lots of time and nothing planned."

The flask made its way back to Ringmatser, who popped the lid open while reaching into another pocket. Like magic, out came a tiny bottle of whiskey and he began to pour it into the flask. He spoke as he poured. "I reckon I'll go back out to the west coast and enjoy the sun. See what an old man like me can do with the rest of his time and money."

Commodore's cheeks started to flush as he stared in anger. "The money we don't have for the show?" he murmured.

Ringmaster smiled and tipped the now full flask towards The Commodore. "Something like that," he chuckled to himself.

Commodore clenched his teeth and looked down into his hands, defeated. "Come now, Commodore," Ringmaster snorted, "Think about how free you'll be! The world is your buffet now."

Before the fight could stir again, Ringmaster stood suddenly and waved a hand over the group. "Well, I believe it's late and we should get some rest if we want to have yet another excellent performance tomorrow. Get your sleep and I will see you all in the morning."

Already drunk, he stumbled off the wagon and out of sight of the Brigade. Commodore shook his head angrily after the footsteps disappeared. "He has some nerve, guys. Some fucking nerve."

The others just stared at their feet and shifted around until it was time to sleep and end the supposed best night of performance in their lives.

CHAPTER 13

Ben woke up early that morning, restless with the heavy thoughts of what was next for him in his new life. He had nowhere to be and nowhere to go. Was it true what Ringmaster had said? If he goes off into the world again, would he be burned at the stake? He didn't know what was true anymore and he hated the thought of having to find out. With an appearance like his, it would be impossible to find work outside of what he already did. Maybe he could work on the railroads or in a factory, hidden under overalls and gloves. He could possibly blend in if he really tried.

He would go back home if he knew where that was, but he didn't have any family. Ringmaster never told him who they were and he couldn't remember anything about his childhood. Judging by the way that the rest of the Brigade reacted to the news that they were being released, he was sure they didn't have any family either.

He rose from his blanket and decided it was best to stop thinking about it for now. There was nothing that could be changed and worrying would only make it heavier on him. He stepped over to the wagon's water basin to wash his face. The water inside it was bubbly and black with Hot and Trot's body paint. He sighed and yelled "Thanks for leaving this shit for me, guys. Go throw this out and get fresh water."

He expected a snarky retort from either Hot or Trot, but he was answered only with silence. He glanced around the sides of the wagon and saw they weren't inside at all. If Ringmaster was up and walking around and saw them outside, they'd be in trouble. Ben realized how silly that was though, considering they were free after tonight anyway. He grabbed the filthy basin and slipped out of the wagon, not caring if Ringmaster caught sight of him either.

The sunshine outside was warm and welcoming on his face as he dumped the black sludge water in the grass a few hundred feet away from the wagon wheels. He thought about how often they had to hide in the wagons so the carnival goers and spectators wouldn't see them before the show. Ben never understood why they had to hide. Ringmaster said it would ruin the illusions, but what harm could possibly be done by a few people who spot them?

Ringmaster also never introduced the main acts to the Throwaways, the local freaks he would hire for the night. They were told not to talk to them or make friends because they would be gone in a few days anyway. He would say that if the show's secrets got out, it would be the end of the act as they knew it and everyone would be back on the streets. Ben knew there weren't any real secrets to the show - just a stage and some props, but he took the Ringmaster's word for it. Mostly because he didn't feel like getting whipped. It didn't matter anymore though. The fact that he was free almost made him smile.

Ben placed the basin down and keeled down into the grass, running his hands across the green blades that tickled his palms. He loved that feeling. *I wonder if I used to do this a lot before this life,* he thought to himself, ripping some of the blades out of the dirt. *Ringmaster always said that I lived in the streets. I probably didn't have the time to play in the grass.*

He eyed the handful of grass for a moment until he

heard a few splashes off in the distance.

He stood back up and walked towards the sound. He wondered if maybe it was an animal playing, or maybe Beatrice came back to speak to him. That thought got him excited again and he quickened his pace towards the splashing.

When he came around to the edge of the forest off of the grounds,he saw Hot and Trot washing their loin cloth costumes in what was either a small pond or a very large puddle. They were completely free of their body paint and their naked bodies were already beginning to burn under the bright sun. Werewolf was lounging in the shade of the trees, eyes half closed and meditative. Ben waved over to them. "Hey, guys. What are you doing? Ringmaster will kill you if he sees you out here."

Werewolf shrugged appropriately and yawned, his mouth agape with nothing inside. Ben always couldn't help but stare into the void of his mouth. He knew that when they weren't on stage, Werewolf removed the fake tongue for the sake of comfort.

Trot continued to scrub at the tiny costume. "Ringmaster wasn't here this morning. Left a note that he was scouting for more Throwaways."

"Really? This early?:

"I thought it was weird too" Hot said from underneath the wet hair she was washing. "Why would he be looking for Throwaways for his last night? We didn't any yesterday."

Trot shrugged in response to her. "Maybe he wants a really big show for the grand finale."

"Yeah. Well, if it's anything like last night's catastrophe, that'll be a sight."

Ben scratched at the giant mole on his face and looked over at Werewolf. "Commodore still sleeping?"

Werewolf shrugged. Hot said, "Haven't seen him either. Maybe he went to do his business. You're more than welcome to go search for him. Mind your step."

Ben knew that Commodore was never up early and he seldom ever left the grounds. But when he did, he never wanted any help from them and would stand and walk in short bursts by himself. He told them he'd rather the pain than the humiliation and Ben could completely understand that.

"Well, I'll see if I can find him, make sure he's okay. I know he's been upset about this whole thing. Probably just needs someone to talk to. I'll be back soon."

Ben ducked under some fallen trees and into the dense woods. After a few hundred feet, he was welcomed with a cool breeze that cut through the branches and leaves. He stepped along a foot trampled path and followed it, listening to birds sing and bugs crick and buzz. He felt bitterness rising deep inside him as he thought about how he had spent sixteen years deprived of all of this beauty.

The wagon would get so stuffy and hot, driving for days without stopping. They'd throw pails of waste out the side and sit in silence, anticipating the night so the air would cool down and the smell wouldn't be so unbearable. Ben shook his head and reminded himself to embrace and enjoy the peacefulness of the woods and forget about harsh realities, if only for a few minutes. Ringmaster couldn't take this away from him anymore and that thought relieved him.

As the brush thickened and the trees grew heavier, he heard sticks and leaves crackling several hundred feet away. He smiled at the thought of squirrels or deer or some woodland creatures near him, being as he couldn't remember what they looked like. The only time he ever got to see those kinds of animals was when they were skinned and cooked. Ben heard Hot talking about how cute and fuzzy live squirrels were and he always wanted to see it for himself.

He slowed his pace down to a slow, soft walk and bent his knees, approaching the center of a giant fallen tree that blocked his view any further He placed his hand on the trunk and quietly rose to see what kind of wildlife was right in front of him.

Instead of a squirrel or a deer, he saw Ringmaster only fifty feet away, shirtless and sweating. His hands and chest were covered in dried blood and beside him was a shovel, dirty and dented with use. Attached to his belt loop was a bloodied machete. He lifted heavy chunks of fat and bone with his hands and dumped it into a dug out hole, each piece falling in with a soft thud. Ben felt his stomach churn and tighten. Fresh, wet meat was piled neared his boots and pooling in a stew of blood. Ringmaster bent and scooped up a few pieces. One of them slipped out of his grasp and fell back to the ground, bouncing with a squishing sound. Ben saw that next to the pile was Commodore's severed head, eyes closed and covered with dirt and dark blood. His black and gold Captain hat was stuffed in his mouth.

"You fat fuck. This is what you got," Ringmaster murmured wildly to himself, throwing the pieces of the man into the hole. He giggled at a particularly wet thud of flesh hitting the dirt. "Look at that, Commodore. You're so fat, you may not even fit in this hole. I don't have fucking time for this. Beelzebub, you bastard, you better be happy. I'm tired of this and I'm walking away, washing my hands clean of it all. You better be good for your word, you tricky bastard."

He continued to babble and murmur and toss the chunks of torso until he was down to the last piece. He lifted the Commodore's head and stared at it silently for a moment. He turned it in his hands a like a ball and studied the clean cut across the neck, admiring his work. "You won't be racking up a food bill anymore, friend."

He dropped the head into the hole and wiped his forehead, smearing blood across his face. "Well, time to clean this up and get back."

He picked up the shovel and began his work on the dirt pile beside him. Ben quickly lowered himself down as Ringmaster turned on his heel to look around suspiciously. A small branch of the tree trunk caught in Ben's trousers and broke off with a tiny "snap."

Ben held his breath, listening. Silence surrounded the two of them for what seemed like several minutes.

Then he heard Ringmaster's boots crunch in the leaves, the step sounding very close.

Ben took off running.

"Ben! Get back here, you son of a bitch! I can explain!"

Ringmaster threw the shovel down and took off after him. "Ben! Stop, let's talk about this! You need to stop! Ben! I swear to God I'll cut your fucking legs off! Get back here!"

Ben never turned his head back. Instead, he dashed and listened to the sound of crunching leaves and sticks start to trail off behind him. He was much faster than Ringmaster and was opening the distance between them. He heard Ringmaster bellow his name and it only made him run faster.

The woods sped past him and he felt dizzy from his frantic pace, losing complete direction of where he was running. He wanted to be back at the camp to warn his friends to run, but his gut instinct told him he was heading the wrong way. The mere thought of guts made his stomach flip.

He didn't see any exit around him, just a blur of green and brown as he weaved. Ringmaster's voice trailed farther and farther back. His legs began to stiffen and grow tired. He wanted to stop, but he knew that would mean Ringmaster was another step closer.

Ben saw a tree trunk with a hollow opening pass by him. He turned on his heels, skidding in the thick leaves and brush, and darted back towards it. He slid into the small crevice and pulled his arms and legs into his chest. He shimmied in and pressed against the back of the trunk, feeling the ants and spiders stir and crawl across his bare shoulders. Closing his eyes, he took a deep breath to soften the pain of the pounding blood rushing through his skull. When the beating slowed and he caught his breath, he heard Ringmaster's desperate calling off in the distance, but couldn't tell in which direction. He sat hugging his body, tears streaming down his face, waiting for his death.

CHAPTER 14

Beelzebub sat upon a jagged, molten rock that glowed red with heat. He perched on the crag, watching the entertainment a few hundred feet below him as he pressed his lips against a long, tarry cigarette. He inhaled and sucked in the white smoke, holding it and releasing it through his nose like a steaming brass bull and laughed to himself at the sight.

A woman screamed and gargled the brown filth of the Stygian marsh she was drowning in right below where he perched. Other women were pushing and scratching each other, shrieking and snagging each others hair while trying to keep themselves surfaced in the dense, foul smelling sludge. "Scratch her fucking eyeballs!" he cried down to them, giggling at the sight. He always loved a good show, especially when the women went at it in the marsh.

One of the women looked up to him and screamed in desperation. "Help me!" She cried to him, fists clenched to another woman's head. She pushed her underneath the black waters to support herself and raise herself up to Beelzebub. He smiled and shook his head, dismissing her with a pass of the hand.

The woman held under the water appeared to stop resisting and went limp. Her body surfaced and the woman who held her down screamed in horror. "Damnit," he muttered to himself. He was disappointed by her giving up the fight so quickly. He knew that she couldn't actually drown and would only be awake again in a few moments to relive the dying all over again, but his favorite part of it was watching the struggle. A soul who gives up so easily is hardly worthy of the rankings of the Brigade.

He flicked his cigarette down into the marsh and realized it was getting late. "Alright, honey. I've got to go."

He stood and waved goodbye to her. She raised her hand and screamed towards him with a shredding, exhausted voice. He giggled. "I've got a new Soldier coming in and I've got to get back to work. I can never catch a break with my man, Tom. Otherwise I'd stick around and see how you do against the rest of the broads."

She slunk down, staring up at his figure so far up away from her. Exhaustion consumed her as her head dropped into the waters and she bobbed, motionless. "Ah, you wouldn't make the cut either, it seems," he said to himself. "Shame, that."

He conjured up his outfit of a white dress and blonde hair and glanced once more at the rest of the drowning women. There seemed to be hundreds of them lining waters, flailing and screaming. He took particular notice to one woman with a plucked out eyeball hanging from her skull. He snorted to himself and waved at them as he made his exit. "Goodbye, ladies. Have fun!"

CHAPTER 15

Ringmaster's voice was hoarse and panicked as he stumbled around the grass. "Ben! Come out, please. I won't hurt you. We can talk man-to-man."

He splayed his arms to balance himself, grabbing onto trees and pushing through the dense woods as he approached Ben's hiding spot. "You've always been my favorite. Did you know that? Come on out, kid. I won't hurt you, I swear it."

Inside the trunk of a tree, Ben held his legs up to his chest and curled his feet. His heart pounded and he knew all he could do now was pray that he was obscured.

"Ben. Be-ee-nn!"

Ben closed his eyes and steadied his breath to keep from panicking. He breathed in and released it silently to calm himself until he heard Ringmaster's boots step in front of the hollowed tree. Ben opened his eyes and saw the bottoms of filthy trousers and the bloody, wide tip of a machete. He froze, unable to move and wanting to scream.

"Ben," Ringmaster pleaded. His voice was cracking in desperation. "Please come out. I have no intentions of hurting you. I just need to explain what you saw."

The silence between them seemed infinite. It continued until Ringmaster cleared his throat and spoke again. "I can't tell you anything if you don't step out though."

The machete twirled and the boots stepped forward.

His feet were right in front of Ben.

"I'm losing my patience."

Ben closed his eyes and pressed his forehead down upon his knees. Ringmaster must know he's here. Now it's just a game. He knew that he was cornered and this was all just for the fun of it. Ringmaster won and Ben lost and this game was just a moment from the end.

Ringmaster groaned to himself. "Fuck," he muttered as he darted past the hollowed tree and sprinted forward, continuing to call out Ben's name. As the sound of the cracking leaves distanced and Ben was left in silence, he felt the adrenaline slow in his body and the real fear start to kick in. Tears rolled down between his knees as he shook and held himself. He wondered if Commodore ever had the chance to feel death as closely as he did or if it was quick and painless. He prayed to God that it was the latter and nothing more.

***

The man in the plain jacket had packed up his fishing gear and looked down at his catch. It was about ten pounds or so, not a bad size for the lake. It had suffocated awhile ago and lay limp. He never kept them in water or tried to keep them alive because he knew there was no point. If the fish were to die, why let it linger and give it hope?

He was still debating whether or not he should start heading towards Kentucky now and be right on the heels of Beelzebub's new man, whoever it was. He was picking up the tracks and could feel the presence, but he couldn't pinpoint this one. He wouldn't be able to pick him out of a crowd, like most of the sinners he was sent to seek. There was something different about this one, and he knew he wouldn't find out what until he was closing in.

Beelzebub was always one-upping him and covering his tracks when he collected his soldiers and Michael could usually figure it out quickly, but this one stumped him. He knew that the new man would have to show his face eventually though and would get cocky quick.

Michael took out his knife and wiped it on his shirt, cleaning it of any specks or lint that may have caught on the blade. He was going to wait a little longer and gut his fish and enjoy the catch God presented him with. Patience was always the best option. So, for now he waited.

***

Ben hid inside the tree for what felt like hours. He wanted to get up and run until he had an inkling of where he was, but one slip up could be death. *God,* he thought. *Where am I going to go? I can't risk being spotted. God help me, please.*

"Hi, there."

A pang of fear gripped him and he clutched his knees closer to his chest. The voice was right next to him. His eyes darted to the entrance of the trunk, but there was no one there. He started to shake, waiting to see Ringmaster's boots step in front of the hollow at any second.

The voice whispered again. "I know you're in there. You don't have to be scared." It sounded soft and sweet like fairy floss and he realized that the voice belonged to Beatrice.

As his pulse slowed, Ben stuck his head out and she stood just off to the side of the trunk, still dressed in her white skirts and loose, bouncing yellow curls. She smiled warmly and Ben felt the fear beginning to melt away in her familiar eyes. She reached a tiny hand out to him. "Don't ask any questions right now. I'll have all the answers once we're in a safe place, okay?"

Ben nodded, put his hand in hers, and pulled himself up. She was surprisingly strong, lifting him in one swift motion. She looked him over and squeezed his hand. "You okay?"

"I don't think so."

"Well, for now you'll have to be - you need to run. Follow me."

She released his hand, turned on her heel, and sprinted in what appeared to be a random direction. Since he had no choice and no idea where he was, he followed close behind, trusting she had some kind of idea better than his plan of hiding until death.

He didn't know how long they ran, but it seemed to never end. He choked and gasped for breath, tired from the fear. He just wanted to curl up in his wagon and go back to sleep as if this whole thing never happened and Commodore was still alive. The memory of the man cut up into heaps was making him dizzy.

They darted between trees, fallen branches, and holes. She was so swift, holding up her skirts, dancing past it all and curving around the downed trees as if she already knew where they were. *It looks like she's done this a thousand times,* he thought to himself.

She turned her head back towards him, hair bobbing up and down as she ran. "We're almost there."

He had no breath to spare for words, so he nodded quickly and continued to follow on her heels, feeling heaviness in his chest and fatigue starting to shroud him. She was not even short of breath, still dashing in full energy. Finally, when Ben felt like he could run no longer, they came upon an opening amongst the trees. She stopped at the edge of it and he skidded to a halt.

The opening in the woods was an agape mouth of darkness. The shadows were thicker and there appeared to be a body of water past their sight. Trees, grass and life all seemed to avoid the area like a poisoned atmosphere. To Ben, it looked almost like some kind of different world beyond the woods. "I don't know if I want to go in there," he said.

"Well, that's a shame because that's where we have to go. Don't be scared."

She stepped through the immense trees and into the mouth in the woods and he blindly followed into the dark circle. As his sight adjusted, he looked up and saw that the lack of light was due to the incredible thickness of brush in the trees surrounding them, yet they stood within a giant perfect circle of dirt and cleared land. The long branches of the circling trees and the woven tapestry of leaves lay like a roof above them. In perfect daylight, it was total darkness in there. They stood at the foot of a long lake, dark with thick murky water that smelled like decay. The area looked like it hadn't been touched in centuries. It seemed out of place, a hole in the center of a dense forest that was blind to the eye past the thickness of the trees.

Ben stared and admired the view as Beatrice stepped away from him. "Do you like it? It's my little home away from home."

Lifting her skirt up to her knees and folding the back of it down under her bottom, she sat down upon a rock at the muddy shore of the water. She kicked off her white slippers and dipped her feet in the mud, wiggling her toes and earthing damp, bubbling sludge with it. She giggled to herself. "Feels good," she said.

Ben's eyes dropped to her. "What are you doing? What is this place?"

She pouted at him and said, "Just taking a rest, giving the feet a breather. Want to sit down with me?"

"Not right now," he pleaded. "Please, we need to go. He's still around here somewhere."

She shook her head and padded her feet in the mud playfully, the sludge bubbling up around her ankles. "Relax, Ben. He's long behind us now. I'm sure that he's back at camp and hitting the bottle as we speak."

Ben noticed her voice didn't have that sweet tone to it anymore, like when he first met her. He stared at her suspiciously as he sat down, his own boots sinking into the mud with a loud squish. "Ugh, this is disgusting."

"Strong words from the Bubonic Boy."

He ignored her sarcasm. "How did you know about Ringmaster? Who are you and what is going on?"

"Well," she said through a growing smile, "I think maybe now is a good time to talk business, seeing how the situation has developed."

"I'm listening."

"I haven't been completely honest with you, I'm afraid. See, I'm the head of a traveling show myself. We used to be one of the more popular shows in the country, but Tom came around and started taking away from me and my poor performers. He stole the bread right out of our mouths and there wasn't a whole lot we could do to stop it. We would try to jump on the local circuits and he was already there, stealing the light with his Devil Brigade, or so he calls it. I wouldn't have minded so much if it weren't for the fact that I knew he abused his performers."

Ben glanced away from her, embarrassed and unsure as to why. "No, he's treated us fine over the years, I guess. He makes sure we're fed."

She laughed and shook her head. "Oh, what a privilege you had. My performers have trailers, feasts of their favorite foods, beautiful costumes, and women whenever they want them. But I'm glad to hear that Tom gives you food every now and again."

She scoffed and Ben sighed. He noticed the pale blue of her eyes seemed much darker now, and somehow more vibrant. He figured that it was probably the lack of any light in the area. "Yes,
he agreed. "I admit it. He's been cruel to us, but it doesn't matter right now. There's a bigger problem here. If you knew I needed rescuing, I can assume you know what happened to Commodore."

She nodded sadly. "I'm afraid I did come across that. It's a shame that had to happen - I bet that chubby guy was a great act, brought in lots of audience.."

Ben didn't know how to respond to her nonchalant tone about it. He remained silent until she continued.

"Instead of having a fate like that poor man who got all chopped up, why don't you do something about this?"

She leaned in closer and whispered in Ben's ear, "I need Tom out of the circuit. If he disappears, I get my audiences back and that means more money in my pocket. If you make sure Tom never shows his face again, not only will you be saving yourself from certain death, I will make you a headline act on my show and the pay will be unlike any you've ever seen."

Ben's stomach churned in horror as he reeled back from her. "You want to pay me to kill Tom? That's insane! I'm not a murderer!"

Beatrice nodded as if she expected such an answer and reached into her blouse. She pulled a one hundred dollar note out from her bra and placed it in Ben's hand.

"What? What is this?" he stammered.

"You'll get one of these every night you work for me. All you have to do is rid the world of the man who brutally murdered your friend. I don't think that this is a complicated choice to make."

Ben stared at the money in his palm. He had never seen a one hundred dollar note before and wondered what he could buy with it. He didn't know the price of many things, but deep down he knew that he could buy mostly anything he wanted with a note this valuable. "You do know that Ringmaster is done after tomorrow night, right? It's his last performance?"

He saw a smirk trail her lips as she looked away from him and said, "He can't be trusted. He says that he's done, but what's to say he doesn't have plans to try and ruin me again? I think it's a ploy to get me off his back, but I am always two steps ahead of him. He just doesn't know it."

"Can't you just talk to him?"

"Oh? Suddenly he is a reasonable man, Ben? You just saw what he did. Make the right choice and, if not for the money, do it for your friend, The Captain."

"Commodore."

"Sure. Commodore, then."

Ben studied the note for a few more seconds, then stuck his arm out to hand it back to her. "No," he said. "I'm sorry. I'm not a killer. As much as I hate Ringmaster, I don't think I can do this."

Beatrice gently pushed his hand back and looked into his eyes. He saw the excitement rising in her and it disturbed him. "Keep that one for yourself. You're going to have to be on your own now."

He wanted to argue and push the money back to her, washing his hands clean of the entire conversation, but he knew that he had to keep it if he wanted to survive on his own. He put the money in his pocket.

"Good," she said as she stood and brushed off her skirt. "If you change your mind, do the deed and find me. I'll be around the area. Just remember, the rewards are more than you'll ever imagine and you may be sparing your friends at the same time. Trust me on this."

Her bare feet pulled out of the bubbling mud and she padded back to the edge of the forest. Ben watched her and realized she left her slippers at the foot of the lake. As he thought to call to her and remind her, she had already turned back to face him. "One more thing," she said. "If you want a safe place to stay until you decide what you want to do, stay here by the water. Nobody will ever find you here."

"Wait a minute," he said. "Why don't you just kill him? Why is this my job?"

She sighed quietly and said, "That's unethical in my line of work. Plus, I don't think the Big Boss would be too happy with me. Be safe, kid."

He watched her walk away among the trees and step out of sight, her pure white dress disappearing out of the shadows of the encircled area. She was gone and he was alone again.

Leaning forward on his knees, he stared into the

dark water. It was filthy, swirled with brown and yellow deposits. *This water is disgusting,* he thought to himself as he reached out to touch it. The smell of ancient earth and dampness was overwhelming and he pulled back. He wondered if it was deep, but it was too dark to see anything beyond the surface.

He began to feel a wave of sleepiness and fatigue. It was sudden and without any kind of control. He thought may the adrenaline had worn him out, but he nodded off on his seat before he could think any more on it, his body slipping off the rock and nestling into a deep sleep.

CHAPTER 16

"Hello, Mrs. Lewis. Thank you for calling me when you did."

He heard footsteps coming down the hall towards his bedroom and it made him nervous. He was wide awake and wondering who would be visiting them right now at such a late hour, especially considering mother never let any strangers into the house. Not after father left them, anyhow. The house was always quiet since he left, no anger and no yelling and no crying. He liked it that way, but would never tell mother that.

A man stepped into his view in the doorway. He had frizzy hair sprouting from underneath his hat. A pair of wire thin spectacles rested on his long nose. He wore a cheap brown suit and carried a medical bag with a red cross on it. He stood next to the boy's mother. He always thought of her as a lovely woman, especially when she wore her pretty green dress, as she did tonight. Her hair was pulled back in a tight black bun and it made her look young, but her tired, wrinkled eyes seemed to give her age away.

The man and his mother stood at the edge of the room and stared at him silently. The boy felt uncomfortable and shifted underneath the heavy blanket on him. To ease the tension, he smiled at the man. "Hello, doctor" he said cheerfully.

No smile was returned and the man seemed to ignore him, turning to his mother as he said,

"You are aware of how contagious he may be if this is what we think it is, ma'am?"

She lowered her eyes sadly and the boy saw her clenching her fists at her side. "Yes, I am now, Doctor. I didn't realize when he first started to show symptoms, though. We don't have many books in the house and I wasn't sure of the signs."

The doctor shot a cold glare at her. "There's no excuse," he snapped. "Please stay out of the room while I get the rest of my equipment. You can talk to the boy from the hallway, if you must."

The mother watched him step out of sight, heavy boots thumping on the wooden floor. As the door swung open and he stepped back out to the carriage, she wrapped her arms around herself and began to shake. The boy knew she was trying so hard to hold her composure in front of him and it weighed heavy on his heart. "Mother," the boy said. "Please don't cry - I feel absolutely fine! Honest!"

She forced a smile on her lips. "Good, baby," she said, her voice shaking. "I'm glad to hear that."

He shot the best smile back at her that he could. "Nothing to worry about! I'll be back on the farm, working in no time. We've got to gather the harvest soon and -"

"No, baby" she said, tears forming in her eyes. "Don't you worry about that right now. Just worry about feeling good. I'm going to be right here for you, no matter what. I'll always be right beside you."

He nodded his head and they remained silent in the confusion of it all. *Why does everyone want to keep me in bed*, he thought. *I feel absolutely fine, same as I did before this whole thing started to happen. Why doesn't Mother believe me?*

His mother's eyes trailed away from him as sound of

the boots returned. She gasped and stepped back, covering her mouth with her hand.

The doctor appeared back in the doorway and the mother stepped away from him in horror. In place of the thin wired glasses was a leather mask with large, circular glass eye holes. They were dirty and fogged, obscuring the mans pupils completely. The front of the mask stretched into a long, narrow beak sealed with metal rivets. Frizzy hair spread out around the mask like weeds from underneath the leather strap that ran across the sides and top of his face. His breath was audible underneath the dense mask as he exhaled heavily.

Pulling the bed covers up over his head to hide himself from the awful costume, the boysaid, "What is that, Mother? Why is he wearing that?"

She winced in pain at her son's desperation, but remained silent, folding her arms across her chest as she looked at her boy sadly. The doctor spoke for her. "Relax, boy."

The voice was muffled and distant. "It's procedure for everyone's safety."

The doctor grabbed the covers with heavy gloves and pulled the blankets away, revealing the boy's naked body covered in black spots and moles. The marks ran up and down his legs, groin, arms, and chest. Shocked and embarrassed, the boy pushed the doctor's hands away and sprung up to his feet to jump off the bed and run away from the horrid sight of the bird man.

A heavy glove snatched the back of his neck before he could get any further. "Stop it, boy!" he yelled. "What is this child's name, woman?"

"Ben," she choked, gripping her shoulders to hold

her own composure. "Please don't hurt him, Doctor."

The doctor threw the boy back down into the bed, the wooden bedpost slamming against the wall. "Don't make this harder on yourself, Ben."

Ben stared into the eyes of the mask. The glass was so fogged and filthy, he couldn't imagine how the doctor could see anything. "I'll behave," Ben said quietly. "Please let go of my neck. You're upsetting my mother."

The glove released his neck and Ben sighed in relief, but his rest was quickly interrupted with another grab, this time on his arm to turn him over to his stomach. Across his back and buttocks were the same black boils and raised skin. Ben thought he heard the doctor chuckle to himself, but it was hard to tell with the mask muffling everything.

The doctor gripped his arm harder and spun him back around, bringing him face to face with the strange bird mask. The eye holes seemed so empty and hollow, like nobody was inside. He could smell some sort of sweet floral scent emanating from the point of the beak. The boy remained silent, afraid to stir until the doctor let go of the boy and he dropped back to the bed. "We're done here. Mrs. Lewis, may I have a word with you in private?"

She nodded, never taking her eyes off Ben as the doctor walked out of the room and past her in the doorway. "Mama will be right back," she whispered. "Okay?"

He watched her arms drop to her sides and her head hang low as she followed the doctor down the hallway. Ben hated to see his mother so distraught. *I wish I could just run up and hug her, tell her I feel fine,* he thought as he crept up from the bed and inched his way to the doorway to listen to their conversation. He pressed his spotted hands against the wall as he leaned in and listened to the doctor.

"Ma'am. I'm afraid it's what we thought all along."

"No. Please tell me it's not. This must be some kind of joke."

"Do I sound like I'm laughing?"

She remained silent.

"Ma'am, that boy needs to be removed from this town immediately. It's for the sake of everyone's health and safety. I'm sorry."

Ben heard his mother choke back a sob. He gripped the wall and bit the inside of his cheek to keep from calling to her. "Then let me go with him," she pleaded. "Please, don't take him away from me. He's my only son."

"Ma'am, don't be ridiculous," the doctor snapped.

"You don't understand. It's okay. I'll get sick with him and take care of him for the rest of our lives. He won't hurt anybody!"

The doctor sighed and clipped his medical bag shut. "You're going to have to cooperate with me, Mrs. Lewis. I'm not going to put you at risk for that kind of silliness. "

He paused for a moment and Ben's legs tightened, ready to run back to bed in case he came stomping back. Instead, the doctor said, "Are you infected, ma'am? Have you shown any similar symptoms?"

"I – I don't think so," she stammered.

"Please, I'm going to need you to remove your clothes and allow me to inspect you as well."

Another pause hung heavy in the air until Ben heard his mother whimper. "There's no need to be ashamed," the doctor laughed. "I'm just doing my job."

"Alright", she responded sadly. Ben heard the dress tumble to the floor and rage welled inside him. He could hear everything just past his doorway: her sniffling and whimpers. The doctor clearing his throat as his hands brushed against her skin. His occasional chuckle and repeated assurances of "almost done." It was only a few minutes, but for every second that Ben could not run out to rescue his mother it was torture.

"Well," the doctor finally said, "You appear to be clear of any symptoms. Put your dress back on. If you want, anyhow," he laughed.

"What now, doctor?"

"As I said before, we need to remove this diseased boy immediately before there's any threat to other folk around here. Two weeks of this is far too long as it is. I'll be taking the boy with me."

She burst out in a loud sob and Ben heard heavy footsteps heading back towards his bedroom. He dashed back to his bed and threw the covers over himself, closing his eyes and hoping that the Doctor thought he was asleep. *Maybe I can stay a little longer if the doctor thinks I'm sleeping*, he thought desperately.

The footsteps stopped at the foot of his bed. "Get up, boy. I know you're awake. Time to go."

Ben clenched his eyes closed harder, listening to his mother sob in the hallway. He thought maybe it was a horrible dream and the doctor and the disease would go away as soon as he woke up. He heard his dresser open and the shuffle of clothes inside it.

"Get dressed," the doctor barked. "You have one minute."

The boy opened his eyes and the doctor threw several shirts and a pair of pants onto the bed. "Can't I stay with mother?" Ben asked, sitting up and staring at the clothes beside him.

"You're trying my patience. Get up or I will drag you out of here naked, child."

Ben looked over at his mother. She held her face in her hands, her body trembling with each uncontrollable sob. The doctor stepped forward and grabbed Ben's ear, pinching it between two fingers and pulling him up. Ben's eyes met with the mask and he could hear the angered breathing radiating behind it. "Now."

Ben jumped up and started to pull on trousers, but before he could get them buttoned the doctor had already grabbed hold of his wrist and pulled him out the doorway of the bedroom. "Momma!," the boy cried. "Stop him, momma! Please"

The mother crumpled to the floor, crying and mumbling undecipherable words into her hands. "Please, let me say goodbye!" The boy screamed as he tugged his arm in the doctor's grip, but the fingers only tightened. His feet dangled beneath him while the doctor pulled the boy along. "Stop this," he grumbled. "You're only making this harder on yourself. Trust me."

Ben stared at his mother, waiting for her to look up from her hands and see her son for the last time. He wanted to see her smile again, like before the disease. That big, shining smile that she used to cast on him when he was young and they played. He wanted to see it just once before he left the house, but she never looked up for the final goodbye, face palmed in her hands as her loud, breathless sobbing continued.

The doctor dragged him out the door of the house and picked up a lantern beside the front doorstep. Ben saw nothing but the black of night surrounding him and his heart began to race. As the doctor raised the lantern and the light cast out, Ben's eyes adjusted to see a black carriage headed by a gigantic dark horse. The creature whinnied and stepped impatiently like a wild stallion, ready to detach from the reigns and take off into the blackened night. The door to the carriage sat open. Ben saw the interior of it: expensive and plush red cushioning, lined with black painted wood. It reminded him of a coffin.

With a swift push into the open carriage, Ben tumbled in and fell face first into the cushion. He climbed upright and turned around to see the doctor remove the plague mask, toss it beside Ben, and slam the carriage door shut.

Ben felt panic surge through his body as he realized that they would be leaving any second. He frantically pulled at the carriage door handle to find that it was jammed tight, hardly budging under his strenuous pull. *The door must be locked from the outside,* he thought. *But how is that even possible?*

He sat himself upright and worked to catch his breath once he realized he was feeling faint. He listened to the sound of the doctor's boots as they rounded the front of the carriage and hopped up into the driver's seat. He waited for the snap of the reigns and for the carriage to move, but fear gripped his heart as he heard the sound of another body climbing up beside the doctor and the seat squeaking underneath their weight. Ben held his ear against the side of the carriage to listen to them speak.

"Happy?" A strange voice said. It sounded deep and throaty.

"He's perfect," The doctor replied. "But, he's not actually sick, right?

"What good would a sick boy do you?"

"Just checking. I was nervous in there!"

"Would I lie to you, Tom?"

"You haven't yet. I think I've got everything I need now."

The whip cracked and the carriage began to move. As the motion built and he swayed in the movement, Ben felt the tears roll down his cheeks. He took the bird mask and held it, staring deep into the glass eye holes and looking at his reflection. The whip cracked again and he hugged it to his chest, sobbing in a way that sounded just like his mother.

CHAPTER 17

Ben awoke suddenly, gasping for breath and snapping his eyes open. At first he thought he was soaked in sweat, but he started to gather that he had fallen asleep beside the lake. His face had dropped into the mud and covered him in sticky, brown sludge.

He sat up and rubbed at his filthy face, feeling the film of mud gather in his hands and fingernails. Glancing around, he felt himself lowering back into reality from his nightmare with the sight of the familiar lake and dense woods encapsulating him, but as the reality set, the anger came with it. *Was that real? My poor mother,* he thought angrily. *Why couldn't I remember this until now?*

The rage boiled within him as he thought of her face buried in her hands and sobbing desperately. He gritted his teeth, the anger shrouding him and shooting pangs of grief and fury through his veins. He grabbed at his hair and grunted, his breath shortening to quick, shallow breaths as the nightmare played over and over in his mind.

Ringmaster will pay.

He looked up to the thick ceiling of branches and leaves. Spots of the sky in sunset peeked through like a mosaic. Ben knew it was getting late and darkness would fall any minute.

He stood up and stared at his mud slathered hands. They shook uncontrollably as his brain gathered where he needed to go. Suddenly, the answer was right there. He knew exactly where camp was and what he needed to do. He broke into a swift run out of the circle and into the woods. Just beyond his line of sight, on the other end of the lake, a young girl kicked her bare feet in the murky water and watched him take off. She splashed in it with her toes as a wicked smile stretched over her lips and Ben dashed out of sight.

***

Ringmaster stumbled around the outside of his wagon, the bottle in his hand spilling with each dramatic swing of his arm. He danced and swayed without a song, gripping the side of the wagon and holding himself up. "No matter what I do, it's always complaints," he muttered aloud to himself, his eyes tracing the ground drunkenly. "I give him soldiers, they're too weak. I give him my best acts, he only wants more blood. It's never good enough."

He took a swig from the neck of the bottle, grimaced at the burn, and threw it to the ground. The brown liquid pumped out the long neck and into the dusty dirt. "He knew my show came first. I'd help out when I could, but he never listens. Just takes advantage of me."

Ringmaster took his hand from the wagon, ready to jump up inside and go to sleep, but as soon as his hand moved he stumbled over his foot and fell on his ass with a loud thud. He felt nothing, and he began to realize just how drunk he was. *Two bottles and I can't feel my body*, he thought as he slumped against the wagon wheel, head lowering into his chest. *Won't matter tomorrow, I guess. Just happy that I don't have to deal with HIS complaints anymore. He's been jerking me around for too long and I'm saying fuck it, I'm retired now. Let him worry about the Bubonic kid in the woods. It's not my problem anymore...*

His eyes shut as his chin buried into his chest and the feeling of sleepiness rushed over him. *I'm retired. No more Devil Brigade, Beelzebub. We're done.*

* * *

The man in the plain jacket packed his fishing gear. He stretched his legs, stiff from waiting for hours. The moment had come and it was time to get to work. His patience had paid off, just as it always did. The time was now and the first battle (of what he assumed would be many) was about to begin.

He took one last glance at the lake. It was serene and peaceful, the vibrant buzz of bugs and flies singing around him. The water sat still, reflecting a pale moon and illuminating the world around him. He knew it was time for him to move on and knelt down beside the water, pressing his hands together and lowering his head. He spoke softly and calmly to himself, his voice humming like decadent musical chords. "Oh Lord, I shall defend all in the battle and in the terrible warfare that we are waging against the principalities and powers, against the rulers of this world of darkness, against the evil spirits. I shall come to the aid of man, whom Almighty God created immortal, made in his Own image and likeness, and redeemed at great price from the tyranny of Satan, I shall restore balance once more. "

His hands clutched tighter and he grimaced shamefully.

"To remove Satan once again will not be the pious route I once had taken. Soul for soul, we must commit to end this War. If I may have to strike down a man for the salvation of all men, so mote it be. I will end this battle how I must. I ask of help against Satan and Beelzebub and all the unclean spirits that wander this world for the harm of the souls. Amen."

He started the long walk to where where he needed to go and he knew exactly where to begin.

CHAPTER 18

Ben had been running for longer than he could remember. The adrenaline and rage kept his legs strong and his breathing steady as he dashed through thick brush and branches. The whip of the passing trees scratched and cut his bare skin, but nothing could take his eyes from the path. Night had already fallen and the air was cooling. His breath escaped with each exhale like a steam engine. *He's a dead man,* he thought with each rhythmic step of his sprint. *Dead man. Tom's a dead man...*

He suddenly had the urge to stop running, his feet planting in the dirt and skidding him to an abrupt standstill. He had no idea what gave him his sudden onset of instinct as his head snapped to the right and he listened for Ringmaster. He turned his body and stepped silently and slowly. Although his chase after Beatrice had brought him to confusing and unknown areas, he was perfectly aware of where he stood and where to navigate. Sounds seemed louder and clearer with every step. Bugs buzzed like sirens and twigs broke like bones; everything had a beautiful song that directed him back to the camp like a compass. He knew that nothing could stop him from getting back to Ringmaster now. Far off in the distance in front of him, a fire flickered like a tiny match in the darkness. It was a campfire. He was almost to the grounds. Ben's eyes narrowed and he stepped carefully, his path set in front of him.

With only a hundred feet between him and the

grounds, he knelt down and crawled along the dirt, watching the flicker of the fire become clearer and the wagons fall into his line of sight. Slouching against the giant wooden wheel was Ringmaster, head tucked into his chest and arms sprawled to the side of him. A bottle of whiskey beside him trickled into the dirt and Ben realized Ringmaster must have nodded off seconds before he got there. A wicked smile crossed his lips as he stood upright, dusted his trousers off, and walked casually up to the unconscious man.

"What did I have to be afraid of," Ben chuckled to himself as he stepped up in front of Ringmaster. He kicked his foot sharply into Tom's side with a loud crack. "You're not sleeping yet, Tom. Get up.

Tom cried out with a gurgling yelp and threw his arms over his head. "Don't! I gave you the fucking Commodore! We had a deal!"

Ben cocked his head, his eyes widening and glaring at the squirming old man. "What did you just say?"

Tom rolled on the ground, holding himself as he cried, "My ribs. I think you broke my ribs...oh god."

Ben knelt down and grabbed a handful of the frizzy hair, reeling Tom's neck back. "Shut up and look at me."

Their eyes met and Ben could see the horror set in as he realized who it was. "Oh, shit. Shit. Kid, look, let me explain."

"Make it fast," he said as he pulled tighter.

"I made a deal with someone years ago, okay? I loved my show and I lost it to debt. I needed a quick fix. He wanted me to do terrible things and I didn't know -"

Ben's anger flared with impatience as he gritted his teeth and twisted his fingers deeper into the hair. "I don't have time for your bullshit, Tom. What did you do to me?"

"What the fuck are you talking about?"

He yelped as Ben tugged his head back in a short snap."You staged as a doctor and stole me away from my mother. Why did you do that? Who are you?"

Tom's eye's widened in fear. "How did - you're not supposed to know about that! Who told you this?"

"Goddamnit!" Ben screamed. He struck Tom's head against the dirt, throwing him down and shaking him violently. "What does that even mean? Why shouldn't I know what?"

Tom gurgled on the vomited alcohol pouring from his lips. "We made a deal, you asshole. We made a deal. We made a deal..."

Ben growled as his hands slipped around Tom's throat and he gripped with all the force in his body. "What deal?" he cried through tears. "What did you do to me?"

Tom thrashed and clawed at Ben's arms and his mouth fell agape, struggling to scream. Ben could feel the resistance in his hands and fought back, leaning his body and pressing all his weight down into his arms. He felt his stomach churn in nausea, but the sight of Tom's bulging eyes and blue face made him grip harder. A vein bulged in Tom's forehead and his eyes rolled back in his sockets. It seemed like hours before Tom's arms went limp and his head slumped back in deadweight. His eyes remained open and stared into the inky black night above.

Ben dropped his hands to his sides and looked over his work, numb and breathless. The face was blue, swollen and motionless. The rage in him faded away and a surge of weakness and horror pulsed through him. "I killed him," he whispered to himself, staring at the dead eyes.

He stood up and crossed his arms as a chill ran through him. He felt completely alone in the world. Just him and the dead man laying before him.

What do I do, his mind screamed. *How do I hide the body? Where is Beatrice? What do I tell the others...*

"The others," he spoke aloud.

He either had to explain what happened, which none of them would believe, or hide the body and run away as fast as possible.

He turned around to scope the situation behind him and saw Hot and Trot, silent and blank faced. It was the first time he had ever seen them completely cleaned of their makeup and he realized how ghostly pale they were. They were wrapped in their blanket and staring at Tom's crumpled body. Tears formed in Hot's eyes while Trot's head nodded slowly, as if he couldn't understand the image in front of him.

Ben spoke quietly and clearly, composing himself. "If Tom had any money, it would be in his wagon. Gather your clothes, get the cash, and leave town."

Trot continued to nod and gently pulled Hot with him back into the wagon. She buried her face in his chest and sobbed. Ben wanted to reach out and assure her that everything would be alright. He wanted to explain the entire situation in one swoop to the two of them, but he knew it was useless. He watched them walk away. Trot whispered, "I don't blame you, Ben", but it was lost in a dusty breeze as they headed towards Tom's wagon.

Ben closed his eyes and pressed his hands against his head. Everything happened so fast and was unraveling before he could devise a plan, yet it seemed like an eternity since yesterday when his life was normal. When he moved his hands from his eyes and blinked, he saw Werewolf standing beside one of the wagons with his fists tight at his sides.

Ben put his hands up, palms facing out towards him. "I'm not going to hurt you," he said. His voice was small and exhausted.

Ben approached Werewolf and watched the furry man's every move. He knew that one wrong move and he would be completely outmatched. With each step he raised his hands a little higher as a sign of peace. "Listen to me, man. I'm going to reach in my pocket for something. Is that okay?"

Werewolf's fists remained tight at his sides.

Ben slowly reached into his trouser pocket and pulled out the hundred dollar note. "Please take this. Get out of here and I will deal with this," he said as he stretched out his hand.

Werewolf slapped the hand down and the money floated to the dirt. An audible growl vibrated in his throat. Ben dropped his arms to his sides and sighed in exhaustion. "Please, Werewolf. Take it. What happened here was personal, between me and him. It's story I can't even begin to start telling, but you have to believe me when I say that he was going to kill me and he probably would have killed you too at some point. Please, let's go our separate ways.

Ben reached for the fallen money to pick it up and offer it again when Werewolf folded his hairy hands together, brought them over his head, and smashed them down like a brick against Ben's back. He toppled over into the dirt face first. Werewolf kicked him frantically in the stomach and legs, each blow as sharp and on point as the last. The wind sucked out of Ben and he rolled out of the way to gain his breath back. Before Werewolf could kick him again, he pulled himself to his feet and leapt, knocking Werwolf down onto his back and falling on top of him. Werewolf rolled himself over and pinned Ben to the ground, his fist pulling back to strike.

Ben could feel the heat of the campfire as it crackled near them and he scrunched his neck to bring his head in, his hair almost catching in the flames. "Stop! I don't want to fight you," Ben pleaded, but Werewolf's knuckles dug into Ben's cheek repeatedly with quick flurries of blows, each shot a blast of searing pain. Dizziness and darkness began to creep over Ben's eyes and with a last surge of energy, he pushed his legs up off the ground and knocked Werewolf off of him and into the campfire.

Werewolf tumbled headfirst into the flames and the bristly hair across his scalp and face lit instantly. The smell of burning hair and flesh melding together caused Ben to retch and roll himself away from the fire. He watched as Werewolf swatted at his face and screamed a guttural, tongueless scream. It was a sickly howl that could be heard for miles as he writhed on the ground. As he smacked at the fire on his melting face, the hair on his fingers and hands ignited and he cried another rasping, helpless howl. Ben froze in horror and watched until it was completely over. Eventually the moaning stopped and all that remained of Werewolf's head was charred flesh. He could still hear the soft sizzling sound of blackened, burnt hairs.

A strong breeze flickered the fire and pulled black smoke out into the sky. The smoke floated into Ben's eyes and he squinted through it. The sight of Ringmaster and Werewolf dead in front of him seemed surreal and out of place. It all circled back to the grim realization that he had become a murderer. The thought gripped him and tears formed in his eyes. If anyone was to find out about this, he'd be executed by dusk tomorrow. He fell to his knees, slumped with his head forward in anguish and exhaustion.

"I understand, Ben," a man's voice said from behind.

Ben's head whipped around to see Trot standing several feet away, fully clothed in trousers and a child's dress shirt, clutching a small bag in his left hand. In his right was Ben's plague doctor mask. He approached slowly, holding it out in offering.

Ben took the mask and fingered the tip of the narrow beak. "Please tell me something," Ben said weakly, his voice cracking. "Do you know anything about me, Trot? Do you know why I'm here?"

"Harry."

"What?"

Trot put his hand on Ben's shoulder. "My name is Harry. And no, I don't. I'm sorry. Find your way home if you can, kid. If you can't find home, then I suggest you not play games with the Devil and you just disappear somewhere. Get lost somewhere in the world and leave all of this behind you. You'll be happier when this ends."

Ben stood up, wiping his tears on his arm. He looked into the eyes of the mask. The glass was years dirty and needed to be replaced. Looking through it tinted the sights beyond, warping and twisting the grounds and the stars. He attached the leather straps of the mask to his belt ring and it hung heavily from his hip like a prized scalp. "Thank you. Be well."

Harry nodded, took one more look at the grisly corpses, and turned towards a hole in the campground fence. Ben watched as the little man stepped past darkened kiosks, food stands, and tiny stages. The lanterns were all out and he soon became a shadow walking through the ghost carnival. Far off in the distance, by the entrance and main road, sat a wooden sign that read Welcome! in big, drippy letters. A small shadow stood as if waiting, and Ben realized it was Hot. The two of them walked off together silently and Ben knew they would have nothing to say for miles to come

CHAPTER 19

"Step right up, ladies and gentlemen. Step right up. Don't be shy. Please, don't be shy.

Tom's throat was dry and bloody, burning his trachea with each word yet he couldn't stop talking. His filthy coat was now seared and burned, melted to the flesh underneath. His arms were attached to long cables that shot up into the fiery, red skies above and they made him gesture wildly, each movement a ripping pain. His legs and torso dangled heavily beneath him and flopped with each motion.

He was bound somewhere between the boiling rivers below and the charcoal and crimson skies above, no sight of end either way. Bite marks and chunks of muscle were missing from his biceps where he tried to chew through them to plummet to his death. He never had enough strength to make it through the tough meat. All he could do was let his weight hang on his burning arms and flail this way and that as the cords shifted and bounced. He wanted to scream or shout or hold his breath until he died but all his lips would say is, "Step right up. Step right up. Don't be shy. Please, don't be shy."

He squeezed his eyes closed, reminding himself it was an awful dream and that all of this pain was some kind of trick. He was in a hellish nightmare and it would all be over soon because they had a deal .

-Yes, we had a deal and you backed out.

He opened his eyes, expecting to see the familiar

speaker, but he still hung there, alone. The cord ripped forward, jerking his arm out of its socket and leaving him dangling by the joint. He grimaced and squeezed his eyes closed again.

-Beelzebub. Where are you?

-I'm just checking in, seeing how you like your accommodations.

-Is this some sort of dream?

-If fire and damnation for all eternity is your kind of dream, then sure. It's all a dream.

-It's not fair. I did exactly what you wanted. You didn't hold up your end of the bargain.

-I don't really care.

He opened his mouth to scream. Nothing but "Step right up" dribbled out.

-Please let me die. Just let it end.

-Afraid not, friend. Pay your dues. I have a new recruit to deal with. You can thank the Bubonic Boy for this one.

-Please. Don't leave me here. Let's make another deal.

He heard a sharp laugh vibrate between his ears.

-I've got bigger fish to fry, Tom. Enjoy your new home.

CHAPTER 20

The night air hung still and dead beside the lake.
The old, earthy water sat motionless as if no life existed
within it. Ben stared at the brown and coagulated mud
centered in the cleared circle of woods where he and Beatrice
first ran to. She told him to meet her there if he did the job,
but she was nowhere to be found. He sat in the mud with his
knees up and his head resting on them. The thought of the
police finding the bodies made his stomach turn. He'd be
dead before tomorrow if they caught him. He replayed the
scene over and over in his mind. *Why did I have no control
over myself*, he thought sadly. *I've never felt that kind of rage
before. What kind of monster am I to kill two men in cold blood?
They'll hang me...*

Behind him came a rustling sound and the pat of
soft approaching footsteps. "I did it," he said quietly.

The footsteps halted and he knew she was caught off
guard. "I know," Beatrice replied.

"I killed Werewolf, too. I didn't want to kill him."

She sat down beside him in the mud and he looked
at her. *She's so calm*, he thought. *It's as if she's done this a
hundred times.*

She smiled at him, her bright teeth shining, as she
fingered at one f the ringlets in her hair. "Sometimes people
get involved in things they shouldn't. It happens. I'm sure
he's in a better place."

He pushed his head down into his knees, sighing in

exhaustion. "I don't understand any of this. Who are you and tell me the truth. I'm too tired for games."

Putting a hand on Ben's knee, she laughed and said, "Well, you've done me a favor. I might as well do you one. To start with, I don't need to tell you that I'm not the head of a show, correct?"

He glanced at the hand uncomfortably and she retracted it. "Yeah, I gather that now."

"Smart lad," she quipped. "I also should not have to tell you that Tom was never any kind of threat to me. I didn't think you were ready for the exact truth yet because I didn't know how well you'd do. I've been interested in you since Tom first found you and I needed to test your strength. What I saw tonight was impressive work and I'm sure the Big Boss will be quite happy, too."

A blank expression washed over Ben's face as he stared silently. She cocked her head, her curly blonde hair titling, as she asked, "No? No questions?"

"Oh," he said, watching her in disbelief, "I've got lots of things to ask. But I have no idea where to begin."

"Ask me one question and I'll answer it honestly and fully. You deserve that much."

"No. I don't want to deal with this cryptic bullshit, Beatrice. This is insanity."

Her eyebrows lowered and her lips twisted into a dark smirk. "Humor me."

"Damnit" He cried as he threw his arms down, hands slapping into the mud. Flecks of it splattered across Beatrice's face and dress, but her smirk never left her face. "I don't know what this is supposed to be, but fine. You want me to play? I guess I have no choice but to play. A question, let's see. A question! What could I possibly ask? How about you tell me why the fuck I'm a soon-to-be-wanted murderer and why you sent me to kill Tom in the first place? How's that? Is that a good enough question?"

His breath staggered and his body shook as he held himself, rocking in his own arms. Beatrice watched him patiently and said, "When you're done having a mental collapse, I can tell you that."

"Oh, God," he whispered to himself, struggling to catch his breath. "This is madness."

Silent and blank, she continued to wait until his rocking stopped and he composed himself. "Alright," she began. "Let's talk about Tom. He was a desperate man with a carnival show that nobody wanted to buy. He catered to an older crowd, refusing to believe that his gimmick went out of style. His thing at the time was trick ponies, cats, dogs, and rats. Nobody wanted to see the animal shows anymore and the spectators became few and far between. The last of his savings were invested and lost in his show. Since he couldn't feed his pets, they all died and he certainly couldn't afford any new animals. He took a job as a scrivener for awhile and pretended that it made him happy for a few decades. He worked his regular hours and lived in his tiny shack and told himself this was what he wanted, but he hated the fact that his dream to be a famous entertainer was now stripped away and so began the drinking.

"One day, he spent his last dollar on a bottle of whiskey and a rope to hang himself with. Before he could go on with his grand finale, he passed out beside the chair. When he woke up, he realized he was so pathetic that he couldn't even kill himself without error. This is where I come in.

"I had been watching him for awhile and I knew

now was the time to swoop in and talk business. We cut a deal within minutes. He could have a show and be a success, but only if he could do some work for me at the same time. A sort of humane service to the world, if you will. I gave him the wagons and props and all the money he needed if he could help me in my mission: ridding the world of sin."

Ben's eyes searched her for any tell of it being a lie and an absurd prank. Her smile and excited eyes told him nothing. "You can't expect me to believe this," he blurted. "What are you telling me here? That you're some kind of deity? What is this madness?"

She held up a finger. "Let me finish the answer to your question. Tom needed fresh acts and something different, and I needed sinners. I asked him what kind of people he despised the most, and you know what he told me? He hated ugly things. Gross and strange looking abnormal humans!"

She paused for a reaction from Ben. He sat and stared, completely detached, so she continued. " I was surprised when I heard this because he wasn't terribly attractive himself. I don't know what his vendetta was, but that was his pick. I suggested we put together a freak show of horrific disfigurement, disease, and ugliness so he could throw the awful creatures to me once he was done for the weekend."

"Throwaways," Ben muttered. "He killed all of the Throwaways."

Beatrice patted Ben on the back with a tiny hand.

"They didn't suffer in their deaths, if it's any consolation."

"Not at all."

"Oh. Anyway, The fat man and the midgets were

easy for him to get. In big cities, they're pretty much a dime a dozen. The hairy guy was a happy accident, you could say, but you were something a little different."

She twirled at another ringlet of hair. "Now, I don't know much about how he got you other than he played doctor or something. Took you right from your mother, I only know the basics."

She's lying, he thought, staring down at his feet to not give her any tells. *She's roping me into something here. She had to know.*

"I don't believe you, Beatrice. I had a dream by this lake last night about my mother and Tom taking me away from her. I hardly find it a coincidence that we meet and suddenly I can remember."

She laughed, her eye's flickering in unexpected excitement. "Well, if you work with me and do what I say, you can coincidentally find out a whole lot more about your family. I can provide you that information."

His heart dropped in disappointment. He already knew he had no choice but to fall into her game. He sighed and said, "Before I make any kind of decision, can you at least tell me why he didn't just kill me and the other main acts of the Brigade?"

"You pulled in too strong of a crowd. He told me you were the best acts he'd ever had and he begged me to let him keep you. He was like a child with a puppy, begging and nagging until I finally said it was okay. By me bending to him, he started to get lazy. Suddenly, the Throwaways weren't coming anymore. He was skipping town instead of killing them, leaving us high and dry. I went months without bodies, waiting patiently but never getting my share. Meanwhile, he was getting more and more popular and I was left with nothing on my end of the deal until I finally got fed up."

"Just, stop, please."

A headache forming in the back of his skull surfaced and left him in pain. *I must be going insane,* he thought as he rubbed at his temples furiously.

"What's wrong?"

"Everything. This is horrific. What kind of monster or demon are you? Why is this happening to me?"

Beatrice reached for the hand on his head and lowered it. She placed two fingers on his temple and gingerly rubbed the throbbing spot. In a flash, the pain faded and he felt fine. "I'm a collector," she said sweetly. "Those freaks were mine to collect because that is what I do, Ben. I'm a collector and I hunt for the worst kinds of humans for The Big Guy. I send them where they belong and put them to work for us and with every body dropped, I make this world a better place."

"The Big Guy," Ben repeated. "You're an angel? I don't know anything about religion other than there's God and angels and devils. I'm sorry if I don't know specifically who you are."

Beatrice's eyes widened. "You don't know anything about God and Lucifer and the Great War? At all?"

"I'm sorry, I don't. Who is Lucifer?"

"Oh, my. Do you know how to read at all?"

"Self taught, but never read the Bible. Mother didn't believe in God at all so she never taught me."

Beatrice nodded and Ben could tell she was surveying the entire situation in a new light. His heart dropped as he asked, "Does this mean I don't get to find out about my family?"

"You still do," she said, still collecting her thoughts. "That's okay. We can work with this. But yes, I'm an angel. My name isn't Beatrice, and I think maybe it's best if I don't tell you my real name so we don't go slinging it around everywhere. People cannot know that I walk the earth otherwise the entire plan is ruined. Is that understood?"

Ben nodded. "So, you're not actually a pretty blonde girl?"

"Afraid not," she laughed. "I do know that you need to stop thinking about me with my dress off, though."

Ben blushed. "You knew about that?"

"I'm an angel, kid. I see shit."

Silence fell between the two of them as the two of them pieced together their own separate puzzles. Ben stared into the murky water beyond their feet and noticed something moving beneath the surface. A few bubbles rippled through the water, then all was still again. "I have another question," he said. "Why did I deserve to be removed? What sins am I guilty of other than having spots on my skin? I don't think I was born this way because in my dream, my mother said that I was only two weeks sick. Why did this happen?"

"That's information you have to earn."

He glared at her furiously. "Why do I have to earn it? Just tell me the fucking truth!"

Beatrice took his hand and placed it in her lap. He watched in bewilderment and tried to jerk it back, but she held on to him tightly. "Because," she said in a soft whisper, "I need you, Ben. You'd be an excellent soldier for us. You can move up the ranks among us, purifying and removing sin from this planet. Send bad souls to Hell where they can be punished." She paused. "Do you know what Hell is?"

He nodded. "Where sinners go to suffer forever. Commodore told me that."

"Exactly. You can remove the hate and pain that plagues this world. The kind of pain that you felt when you found out what Ringmaster did to you and your mother. You'll have me to help you and protect you.

"I'm the ugly sinner you wanted Tom to remove. Why do you want my help?"

"You were, but I can change that. You've proved your worth and I can help you. I have more power than I think you'll ever know."

Her hand rubbed at the black spots on his skin and he felt his fingers tingle and burn. He tried to pull away from her, but her grip was too strong to fight against. The burning was unbearable and he cried out in pain. "Let go!"

As if on cue, she opened her hands and his arm jerked back. He blew on his fingers to cool them down. "What the hell was that?"

"Look."

His hand and fingers were a healthy, glowing pink, devoid of all boils and marks. His eyes widened and he stared at the plain skin in disbelief. "Can you do this to my entire body?"

She smiled. "I can. You're a handsome boy and you'll be even more handsome if you agree to help me. You've got what Tom didn't have - desire. He grew lazy over the years and comfortable. I know you won't because you've never had a second chance before, let alone a first. You'll be a beautiful angel walking an awful world, which is yours to sweep and clean as you wish."

Ben flexed his fresh, pale fingers. "An angel. How would I know who to remove?"

"Well, tell me something. What sin would you like to rid the world of?"

His eyes became fixed on the waters again. It started to dredge and stir, forming curvy outlines that blended and mixed together deep under the surface. They were feminine figures, silently moving back and forth amongst one another and churning the brown and dark waters like a filthy watercolor painting. The long shapely legs and hips swirled, an orgy of browns and blacks and yellows.

"All of it," he replied. "I want all of the evil gone."

Beatrice laughed and stood up, the bottom of her dress covered in mud. "That's enthusiastic of you, Ben."

"I'm serious."

He stood beside her and brought his face close to hers. He could see the fire burning in her eyes. It was far away, but the flicker was there. "I'll do your work if you tell me who I am, right now. I want to know everything about me. I want to know my family, my friends, where I'm from. I want to know why I can't remember anything."

She shook her head sadly at him. "That's not how it works, friend. Bring me your first soul and then I'll tell you what I think you're ready to hear. Or you could spend the rest of your life an unloved freak with no story to tell and you'll die somewhere in the streets. The choice is yours and personally, I think it's a simple one to make."

She stepped into the murky water and waded ankle deep, mud bubbling beneath her feet. The curving water seemed to retract away from her and circle around her. "I think you and I could do some great work together, Ben. I'll make you an Angel and take you away from this awfulness. Just think about it."

She waded further in until she could swim out

towards the middle of the lake, the shapes and figures squirming around her. She kicked as she swam, stirring fiery and filthy colors. Her dress was completely brown now, finally stained from the dirt.

Ben called out to her before she was completely submerged and said, "Beatrice! Are you really an angel?"

She laughed and yelled back, "I am, but all you really need to know is I'm the only chance you're ever going to get. I'll see you around, Ben!"

She ducked her head underneath the water and within a few moments the stirring and swirls subsided into calm and stillness. Ben waited a few moments to see if she'd resurface and she didn't. He stepped back into the dense woods, now silent under a pale moonlight, his mask bouncing against his hip, reminding him of everything he didn't know.

CHAPTER 21

A man sat on a train, eyes sleepily closing to the rhythm of the steam driven engine. He was an older gentleman, dressed in a sharp suit with expensive dark shoes and hat to match. His clean, dark hair was slicked back with greasy pomade. A heavy mustache hid a small smile on his face as he started to fall asleep.

He was thinking about his wife at home, the beautiful little dear he loved so much. He had been away on travel for a week and couldn't wait to climb into bed with her and remind himself of what she felt like. His smile widened at the thought of her tiny, naked body and he adjusted himself in the train seat, unbuttoning his vest and drifting off. He knew that sleep would unwind him for the next few hours and he'd be home soon enough.

"Mind if I sit here, sir?"

The voice was right beside him. Sighing, the man kept his eyes closed and waved his hand lazily. He felt the seat cushion press up as someone sat next to him and shifted around a bit.

"Thank you, sir. Mighty kind of you."

He nodded again and pulled his hat over his eyes.

"Going home, sir?"

The man sighed again, this time dramatically, and opened one eye to see a young man with shaggy dark hair smiling happily at him. The boy couldn't be more than a late teenager, he suspected. He glanced up and down to gather the status of the boy: nice slacks, new shoes, clean skin, and a pressed shirt. "Yes, lad," he responded. "Going home to Baltimore. You?"

"Aye. Well, no. I don't live in Baltimore, but I have to visit for work. So yes, going to Baltimore."

"I see."

The boy leaned back in the seat and crossed his legs. His foot shook in excitement. "Heard it's a beautiful city."

"Yes. Definitely a sight if you haven't seen it. Well, I need to get some sleep before I get home, son. So, I must say goodnight now."

With that the man smiled politely, closed his eyes, and ended the chat.

The boy nodded. "Yes. Very good."

They sat in silence for only a few moments until the boy blurted out again. "Tell me, have you got a wife, sir?"

"Yes, boy."

"Very nice. I don't have a wife or girl myself. Never had the chance. Too busy, you see."

"Quite."

"Yes. Don't even know where my mother is, I'm afraid. No women in my life."

The man grunted impatiently. "Sorry to hear that, lad. I need sleep, if you don't mind."

"Oh, right. So sorry."

The man took a deep breath and before he could try to start focusing back on his rest, the boy spoke again.

"Is she lovely, sir?"

The man furrowed his eyebrows and snatched his hat from over his eyes. He sat up and glared at the boy, who smiled at him innocently. "Excuse me? What did you just say?"

The boy 's eyes and smile widened. "I just want to

know if she's a pretty little lady, sir. No harm meant by it of course."

"What business is that of yours? I'm trying to take a nap here and you continue to pester me and bother me with silly questions? If you can't keep quiet, then simply move. Good day to you, lad."

The boy nodded. "So sorry to bother you, sir. I will leave."

The man rested back in his seat and closed his eyes again, now irritated and unable to sleep.

"Just one more thing, Mr. Kane."

The man's eyes opened. The boy was standing face to face with him.

"Does your wife know how many women you've raped and tortured?"

Before the man could feel his heart drop, a small, sharp knife crossed his throat and the hot blood cascaded down his dress shirt. He would have screamed, but he was dead before he could open his mouth.

Ben tossed the small knife into a bin near the body and looked over at the others on the train. The passengers slept peacefully, unaware of the slouched, bloody corpse or the boy who took a seat across from it and watched the blood pour. When the flood began to bubble and slow, he drifted to sleep while unconsciously fingering at the long-beaked bird mask stuffed in his canvas bag. He had a few hours until Baltimore and he had someone he had to meet with.

CHAPTER 22

Stepping off the train into the frantic station was almost impossible. The police, dressed in all black uniform with silver buttons, pressed through everyone to get through the train door. Ben kept his eyes down, frowning in sadness, so the police would step by and not interact with him. He overheard one of the men say, "How could a man be killed in cold blood and nobody saw it?"

"A shame," a young girl said beside Ben. "Poor man had his throat slit right open. What could have possibly happened?"

Ben shrugged, keeping his eyes lowered. "Damn shame," he muttered. He was trying to listen to the police near the body.

"Wait a minute," another policeman said. "This is Alexander Kane."

Silence hushed over the entire train and Ben had to force a smile off his face.

"Oh my," the girl next to him said. "That's the man wanted for rape. To think I was sitting near him. Oh my God." Tears formed in her eyes and Ben whispered back. "He's gone now. Don't fret over it. You're safe and that's what's important."

The girl looked up at him and nodded, wiping her eyes. "Thank you. You're very kind." Her eyes traced him up and down and he realized she was checking him out. *She got over it fast*, he thought to himself, shooting a smile back at her and a nod goodbye before he wrestled off the train and into the station. He didn't want to stick around for the questioning and disappeared into the crowds of folk, most of them dressed in fine dresses and suits, waiting to get on the train.

***

Beatrice had told him to meet at the Baltimore Federal Building. It was described to him as the biggest building in town and that she would be right in front of it. Ben walked through the hot summer heat, sweating from the dirt rising in the streets and the constant movement of fast paced bodies around him. As he approached the building, he fanned himself and looked around for the curly blonde hair and cherub face, but she was nowhere to be found. The only person in front of the building was an old and ragged beggar, his white wiry hair popping out from his skull. His clothes were filthy and covered in mud. In front of him was a glass cup and a sign that said:

The End is Nigh. Ask Me Why.

Ben approached the old man and dropped a coin into the cup. "I don't want to know what the end is nigh", Ben said, "But you should get yourself a beverage, sir. It's hot out here today."

The old man smiled, a toothless and rotten mouth exposed behind his cracked lips, and grabbed the note from the cup. "Bless you, child," the old man cackled. "Good job on the train today."

Ben startled and stepped back, staring at the old man in fear until it slowly pieced together in his mind.

"Damnit, Beatrice," he muttered, putting a hand to his chest. "You scared me to death. Why this get up?"

"Because a little blonde girl walking the streets of Baltimore alone may not be in my best interest. Today, I'm one of the mix – just an old beggar with a clever sign that everyone will ignore."

"Right." Ben looked around at the bustling men and women around him. The women picked up their skirts and dashed along to keep up with the men in black suits and bowler hats. "So, what do I call you today, since you're obviously not a Beatrice anymore?"

The old man cackled. "I don't have a name right now. Nobody has asked except you, therefore I don't need to make one up today."

"I see. You know, I liked you better as a blonde."

"Why don't we just call me Bub from now on."

"Bub. What a silly name."

Bub cackled in laughter again, this time loud enough to call attention from a few of the passing men. They grimaced in disgust and carried on past Ben and Bub. "Stop it," Ben snapped. "You're making a commotion. I'm already a little worried about this morning. The police got in the train before I got off and I don't want to be brought in for questioning."

Bub ignored him and pointed to his sign.

The End is Nigh. Ask Me Why.

"Nobody has asked me about this," he said. "I am the only person on this earth right now who has the answer and nobody seems to care. If they would just give me a quarter, I'd happily tell them why the end is nigh. Nobody listens, nobody cares. Just goes about their way. But you, Ben, gave me a coin, so you must want to know the answer."

Ben felt the anger rising inside him. "I told you I didn't. But, I do want to know more about my family now."

"You really want to know?" Bub's voice was low and serious for the first time.

Ben's heart skipped a beat. "Yes. Tell me, please."

"Nope! Thanks for the free money!"

Bub waved the coin around like a flag and cackled heinously. Ben watched in disgust. "What kind of angel are you," he snapped. "Angels are supposed to be good and you've done nothing but torture me!"

The money stopped waving and Bub's arm dropped as he stared at Ben. "Do you wonder if you've made the right choice, kid?"

"What? What do you mean?"

"I mean you're going to find out some very awful things about yourself and the life you lived. Do you really want to know the truth or do you want to keep living in blissful ignorance?"

Ben's patience wore thinner and thinner. "Why does this have to be a game?"

"I'm just looking out for you, friend. There's going to be a lot of sadness to uncover and I'm not sure you're ready for it."

Ben stepped in close and knelt down beside Bub, his voice dropping as he said, "I just committed my third murder within two days. You don't think I'm ready for this?"

"I noticed that wasn't exactly a hard task for you. I know you're stronger than I originally thought, Ben. I have a lot of faith in you, but something tells me that you might get too ahead of yourself and not be patient."

"How so?"

"Anger's a bitch, kid. Be too hasty and you get no answers. A little fear can bring out the truth in some of the most unexpected people."

Sighing, Ben shook his head. "Well, what's next?"

The old man ignored him and snatched his cup off the ground, shaking it at a woman passing by. "The end is night, ma'am! I can tell you why for just a coin!"

The woman stared forward as she lifted her skirt an inch and walked faster. He shook his head and smirked at Ben. "Everyone is too uptight here. Especially you, friend. Ever heard of pleasure with business?" He laughed again.

Ben grabbed the old man by his shirt and lifted him up from the ground, his feeble legs dangling. "Stop testing me. I did the work and now I want answers. That's why we're here. Who do I have to collect next to find out where my mother is?"

The old man cried out and yelped, "Help me! Help! This boy is crazy! Get the police! Please!"

Ben turned his head and saw a gathering of a few men watching him. One of them, an older man, reached out to grab Ben's shoulder. "Get off him, lad! Let the old man go!"

He released his grip and Bub collapsed to the ground in a loud thud. He heard Bub chuckle under his breath. Ben eyed the man and put his hands up innocently. "Look, this doesn't concern you," he said. "I'm not going to hurt this man. Please leave us alone."

The stranger glanced at the boy up and down and walked on. "Are you crazy," Ben started. "Do you want the police to -"

When Ben turned back to Bub, he was already gone.

The only thing left on the sidewalk was the empty cup, the sign, and a tiny folded up map. Ben knelt down and unraveled it to see the image of New York state imprinted on it with hundreds of roads and lakes and valleys. And in between all of the landmarks was a little black circle drawn in ink.

CHAPTER 23

"I've never ridden in an electric car before!"

"Is that right? Well, you're quite in luck!"

The driver turned his head to smile at the woman beside him. He was a young man with a strong jaw and prominent blue eyes. He wore an expensive and soft coat lined with rabbit fur and a short cap over his wavy, trimmed hair.

She laughed and watched the trees and grass and scenery pass by them. They weren't moving very fast, but to her it seemed as if they were flying, feeling the bumps bounce them around in the cushy, plush car seat. She adjusted her black feathered hat and veil pinned to her thick, brown hair after one particularly large bump set it off balance. She giggled and put a gloved hand on his shoulder to steady herself. "I've only been in a carriage before, but the roads never feel this bumpy. Why is that, Henry?"

"We're traveling at almost twenty miles per hour, my dear. It's going to be a bit of a rough course."

"How do you know how quickly we're moving?"

He pointed to the gigantic dashboard behind his steering wheel. "See that little plate in front of me with the numbers? And that little stick pointing to the twenty, yes? Well, that's our speed. Very neat, huh?"

She nodded and smiled. "You sure do know a lot about cars!"

"I like to think I know a thing or two. When you

spend the money I did on this beautiful piece of machinery, you feel almost obligated to do a bit of research. Practically had to sell my soul to get her to the US!"

The road was starting to become muddy and rockier as they headed north through New York. They were traveling to Collingwood Opera House to see *H.M.S. Pinafore*, one of her favorite plays that she loved to sing. She had seen it performed everywhere except in Poughkeepsie, she said. With that, he made sure to reserve grand, private seats and they were off. He loved to buy her whatever she desired, mostly because she refused to accept it most of the time as if she were being coy. This was the first gift she ever gladly submitted to in the few months that he had courted her.

"Will you sing me a bit from the show, dear? What's that song you like?"

She shook her head bashfully. "I hate being put on the spot."

He patted her hand and said, "Shy in front of me? Really? Come on now, I would love to hear it. You sing it so much better than them."

"Which one?"

"That pretty one, about Heaven."

She giggled and breathed out slowly. With her next breath, she began to sing in a soft, whispy baritone:

Fair moon, to thee I sing,
Bright regent of the heavens,
Say, why is everything
Either at sixes or at sevens?
Fair moon, to thee I sing,
Bright regent of the heavens...

Henry loved her voice. He knew it was probably the reason he still kept her around for this long. He always loved a good song and she knew so many and sang them well. He gently braked as he rounded a corner on the road, the mud getting slippery beneath the wheels. He listened to the soft rasp of her voice, feeling it excite him. "My dear, I may not be able to control myself if you don't stop singing now..."

She smiled at him. "Maybe I don't want you to control yourself."

Glancing her up and down with a smile, he watched her chest rise with each breath. "Well, then..." he said as he pulled the car over to the side of the road and put it in park. "This isn't exactly appropriate for a lady of your caliber, you know."

"When have you ever cared about appropriate, Henry?"

He laughed and gently pulled her towards him, kissing her neck and chin. As his lips traced the cloth over her nipples, she sighed and ran her hands through his hair, biting her lower lip. As he lowered his face to her stomach, kissing her with each movement, he felt something cold and heavy touch the back of his neck, and then she screamed. Henry sat up quickly to see a man holding a heavy Winchester aimed right at his eyes. The length of the shotgun pressed against the side of her neck and the barrels right in his face. "Oh my god," Henry whispered. "What do you want?"

The man did not say anything, but instead pushed the barrels against the bridge of Henry's nose. His breath staggered. "Sir, please. If it's money you want, just take it," he said.

The man spoke. "I don't want your money."

"What is it...the car? Have the car. Take it, just take it," Henry stammered. "Please. Whatever you want. Just don't kill us."

"I want the girl."

She whimpered and shifted her eyes to him, wide and fearful. He smiled at her.

She lunged her body towards the door handle. Before she could wrap her hands around it he said, "Stop it or I'll kill you."

She froze, not moving an inch. "Step out quietly," he said. "Don't try to run because I will catch you, either myself or with a bullet."

Her body shook as she slowly opened the door, her stare shooting back and forth from Henry to the gun. Henry said nothing, only watched her as she stepped from the car and walked around the front, her heels clicking in a loud echo across the vacant road. She stood several feet away from the man with her hands above her head. "Who are you?" she whispered.

"Michael. That's all you need to know."

She stared wildly and Michael could see in her eyes that she was debating running. Although he was sure he could catch her, he knew that a tiny woman like that could get a head start that would make the chase harder. He wasn't in the mood for a game tonight.

She yelped in surprise and cowered down as he stepped to her and grabbed her forearm. His grip was remarkably strong and with a tug, her legs kicked out from under her, causing her to stumble and hang her weight in his hand. He lowered his arm down, dropping her into the dirt and onto her knees. She began to wail, crying and begging between inaudible words and loud gasps. The man looked back up at Henry, who sat in the car with his hands on the wheel, terrified. "Will this be a problem?" the man asked. His voice was empty and emotionless.

The barrels of the shotgun were now pointed down on her blonde scalp. "I don't think I have a choice," he whispered.

"You never asked if you did have a choice. You only assume."

Henry's eyes widened. "What? What kind of madness is this? What do you want?"

"Are you going to try to save her? Maybe plead with me a bit? Anything?"

Henry remained motionless, his hands gripping the wheel. "I'm too scared."

Michael pressed the gun down into her hair and she cried out. "I have two shells in there and one of you is taking both of them. Is it her or you?"

Henry sat still. Michael's eyes pierced through him. "You're not very much of a man, are you?"

"I...I don't know her that well."

"I do. She's innocent."

Henry's knuckles were white and his breathing heavier. "Then why hurt her?"

"Because somebody needs to go to Heaven tonight. It's the balance of things. Is it you or her? Make the choice."

"I will not."

"You just did."

Henry never saw the shotgun blast. The sound exploded in his ears and the blood splashed up on the car door and in eyes. He fell backwards across the seat and covered his face, shaking and holding himself. Beneath his fingers he could feel the spots of wetness and hard pieces of skull. He screamed and sobbed, running his hands up to his hair and gripping tightly, spreading the gore across his face.

"All you had to do was speak up," Michael said. "This is your sin to live with. You're one of Satan's men, not mine. She will be in Heaven and you'll never see her again, as God has instructed."

The man slung the Winchester back over his shoulder as he stepped over the remains of the girl. He wiped his shoes in the road and kicked the blood off his pant leg and carried on. Beelzebub's man would be in New York any day now and he had a lot to prepare before they met.

ABOUT THE AUTHOR

Toni Odell is an author, editor, and television production freelancer from upstate New York. She graduated from SUNY New Paltz with a major in Creative Writing. During her years of study, she co-founded the e-zine Otherwise Caffeinated. She currently lives in Wappingers Falls, NY.